the class

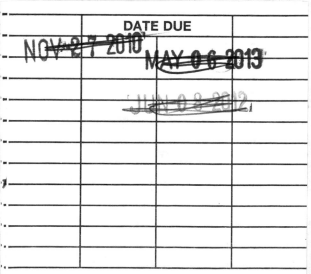

3-09

the class

François Bégaudeau

Translated from the French by Linda Asher

Seven Stories Press
NEW YORK

3-09

18-

Seven Stories Press
140 Watts Street
New York, NY 10013
www.sevenstories.com

In Canada: Publishers Group Canada, 559 College Street, Suite 402, Toronto, ON M6G 1A9

In the UK: Turnaround Publisher Services Ltd., Unit 3, Olympia Trading Estate, Coburg Road, Wood Green, London N22 6TZ

In Australia: Palgrave Macmillan, 15–19 Claremont Street, South Yarra, VIC 3141

College professors may order examination copies of Seven Stories Press titles for a free six-month trial period. To order, visit www.sevenstories.com/textbook or send a fax on school letterhead to (212) 226-1411.

Book design by Jon Gilbert

Title page image courtesy of Sony Pictures Classics

Library of Congress Cataloging-in-Publication Data

Bégaudeau, François, 1971–
[Entre les murs. English]
The class / François Bégaudeau ; translated by Linda Asher. -- 1st English-language ed.
    p. cm.
ISBN 978-1-58322-885-2 (pbk.)
I. Asher, Linda. II. Title.
PQ2702.E34E5813 2009
843'.92--dc22
                                    2009002345

Printed in the United States of America.

9 8 7 6 5 4 3 2 1

Translator's Note

The school pictured here lies in a lively *arrondissement* notably mixed in language as well as in race and class. As dialect renditions can be oppressive to read over the length of a book, I have merely sketched the speech styles of the speakers and then left them to communicate in ordinary language. An occasional omission in the English occurs where the original lines turn largely on a problem in French sound.

The narrator here teaches French language and literature, and serves as head (homeroom) teacher, to one middle-school class of fourteen-year-olds. The class moves as a group through other teachers' rooms for other subjects.

A coordinator/supervisor (called a CPE in France, and here referred to as "dean of students") acts as go-between among students, teachers, and principal. In American schools, this role, and that of the "bursar," might fall to assistant principals or guidance counselors.

The class is described here as being in ninth grade; this is the last year of middle school, which may end with a *Brevet* exam that partly determines placement in the *lycée* or high-school level. This final year of middle school is known—in France's reverse counting system—as *troisième*, and is followed by the *seconde*, a link year during which students begin vocational training (*lycée professionel*) or courses in preparation for an academic baccalaureate program (*lycée général* or *technologique*).

Three days before, I had unsealed the envelope with a feverish fore-finger. Barely glancing at the first page, I went on to the second, darkened with a rectangular table divided into some fifty boxes. The columns for Monday, Tuesday, Wednesday and Thursday were variously filled out, with Friday's left untouched, as I had asked. On the school calendar stapled to the two sheets I counted thirty-three working weeks, which, multiplied by four, minus holidays and plus an estimate for related meetings, gave me the number of days my presence would be required. One hundred thirty-six.

twenty-five

On the appointed day, after coming out of the metro, I stopped at the brasserie to avoid being early.

At the copper counter, the uniformed server listened with one ear to a fellow in his forties whose bespectacled eyes zig-zagged down a newspaper article.

"Fifteen thousand less old folks, room for the young."

The two hundred fifty yards still left to go would take me two minutes, so I waited till a minute before nine o'clock to set off. I slowed outside the Chinese butcher shop so as not to overtake Bastien and Luc, shaking hands at the end of the street. After the corner, I could no longer avoid them as they joked with a monitor before the huge door, its solid wood panels opened onto the lobby.

"I had a vague hope the whole place would've burned down."

"I suppose you'll say it's too late to set a bomb."

I left their snickers behind me. The summer construction wasn't finished, and blue-overalled workers were moving from the tiled playground into the interior court with long narrow beams on their shoulders, setting them upright against one of the inner walls.

The door to the staff room had been brightened up with blue

paint. Gilles was pacing around the oval table away from the others, a forbidden pack of cigarettes in his hand.

"Hey."

"Hey."

Scattered among the gray armchairs in the lounge corner, the new teachers listened to Danièle as she tried to relax them. I took a seat in the ragged circle, the edge of one buttock on the table holding the coffee machine. One thirty-something woman was the most talkative.

"Anyhow, I knew that coming back intra-muros I was taking that risk."

She raised the stakes.

"Intra-muros—gotta say that fast. Could go either way."

People were silent, waiting to see.

Coffee cups into the trashbasket, we moved toward the study hall, where the principal hoped that we'd had a pleasant vacation. The audience murmured a Yes pointedly colored with regret that it was over. The principal said Oh well what can we do, then cleared his throat to change registers.

"Although half of you are joining us for the first time this year, you all know that there are middle schools more restful than ours. You will see that the students here do not lack for spontaneity. Some, in fact, are extremely spontaneous."

Leaving it to his listeners' throat-clearings to comment on the euphemism, he invited people to introduce themselves. We stood up in turn to tell what school we had come from or how long we'd been at this one. We'd been here for fifteen, ten, five, two years, or we had come in from the suburbs. We were named Bastien, Chantal, Claude, Danièle, Elise, Gilles, François, Geraldine, Jacqueline, Jean-Philippe, Julien, Lina, Luc, Leopold, Marie, Rachel, Sylvie, Valerie. We were awaiting our final schedules.

When they had been distributed, few shouted with joy. We went back into the staff room to consult the lists of students in the classes we were assigned. For the sake of the newcomer called Leopold—thirties, right eyebrow pierced with a ring—Jean-Philippe, on the job four years already, slid his finger down the list of names in a seventh-grade class, at each one remarking "nice" or "not nice." Leopold did the accounting in his head.

Dico hung back from starting up the stairs after the other students.

"M'sieur I don wanna be in this class it really stinks."

"Why does it stink?"

"And besides, you for homeroom teacher that's no good."

"Get going."

Most of the students were waiting for me in front of a room on the second floor. Frida now had long hair and red letters spelling GLAMOUR appliquéd on her black T-shirt. The students settled into the creaking chairs according to their affinities from the year before. The four Chinese girls took the two first rows against the right-hand wall.

"Sit down and be quiet."

They sat down and were quiet.

"To make things clear from the start of the year: I want people to get in order immediately. Five minutes lining up downstairs plus five minutes coming up the stairs plus five more to get ready, already we lose a quarter of an hour of work time. Just figure what that comes to, a quarter-hour wasted per period over the whole year. If we have twenty-five periods a week and thirty-three weeks, that makes over three thousand minutes wasted. There are some middle schools where they work a full hour per hour. Those schools—you start off three thousand minutes behind them. And then we're surprised."

Khoumba, pink plastic earrings, didn't raise her hand before speaking.

"M'sieur there's never an hour, every period is, I dunno, fifty minutes, never an hour. Like here we start at 8:25 and the first lesson ends at 9:20, that doesn't come to an hour."

"It comes to fifty-five minutes."

"It's not an hour, you said it's an hour but it's not an hour."

"Yes well all right, the important thing is that we waste too much time, and now again we're wasting it. Take out a sheet of paper and fold it in half."

They wrote their last names, first names, addresses, and other information, all completely available elsewhere. Mohammed did not understand.

"M'sieur why you asking for this? We already give this stuff to the student dean guy and all."

"Yes but this is just for me."

With the sole purpose of delaying the moment when we would

get into the actual subject, I asked them to write a ten-line self-portrait. I wrote the term in chalk, hesitating over the hyphen. Amar asked if he could do an imaginary self-portrait.

"If you like, but I'd rather have your real portrait."

"Can I begin with My name is Amar?"

"If you like."

Khoumba did not raise her hand before speaking.

"M'sieur, I'm not gonna put My name is Amar, I'm gonna put My name is Khoumba."

"You being smart?"

She hid a smile as she bent her head over her paper, she had a red clip stuck on top of her skull. Somebody knocked and the principal appeared in the doorway, followed by the bursar Pierre and the two main deans, Christian and Serge. Since the students had not done so on their own, he asked them to rise.

"It's just a way of greeting an adult walking into the room, that's all. It shouldn't be seen as a humiliation."

On the low table in the lounge corner, Bastien had left a packet of cookies meant for everyone. Danièle chose one.

"I'm telling you, if you really take the time to exhale, with each breath you drop down another step toward sleep. The point is to yawn. I know what I'm talking about, I used to do relaxation therapy. Before, I would sleep maybe two hours a night, now I'm practically turning into a narcoleptic."

Lina plunged a hand into the open packet next.

"You have some trick for a bad back?"

"Same thing—relaxation techniques."

"Because this back is impossible."

"With me it's mainly headaches."

"I'm telling you, relaxation techniques."

A bald baby smiled, taped inside the locker door of the woman named Elise, who was looking over her schedule again.

"Three periods Friday afternoon, thanks a lot."

"I got the same thing Thursday."

"Yeah but still Thursday is better."

"Yeah but starting at eight Monday morning, no leeway."

"Yeah but at least the kids are still asleep, it's calmer."

The newcomer Geraldine straightened up, parallel to the woman with the parasol in the painting behind her.

"Anyone know how to get the copy machine to do both sides of the page?"

Bastien spoke for everyone.

"Um—nobody knows how, but there are cookies here if you want one."

"The bell ring?"

Asking the question, Lina knew very well that it had. So did Danièle.

"You sleep better, it changes everything."

They gave me the silent once-over. I forced myself not to smile.

"So that's it, you write your own self-portrait. You've got five minutes to do ten lines."

A boy with a shaved head raised his hand. Thanks to the folded sheet upright at the edge of his desk, I could identify him: Souleyman.

"Why we doing this?"

"I have all my classes do it."

"They's no point."

"The point is getting to know you."

And stalling at the beginning of the year.

"But we don't know nothing about you."

I wrote my name on the board. They copied it into their home-report booklet. I absentmindedly stepped back a few feet to see whether it was straight. A kid with the name Tarek written in blue marker letters on his folded sheet had his hand up.

"M'sieur are you a teacher that does a lot of dictations?"

"What do you advise? Should I do a lot or not a lot?"

"I dunno, you're the teacher."

"In that case, I'll give it some thought."

A short dark-haired boy in the front row had already turned around in his seat three times. After a glance at his folded sheet, I was able to call him by his first name.

"Mezut, it's me you watch."

He didn't seem to hear.

"Mezut, it's me you watch, yes or no?"

He mumbled an unconvinced Yes.

"Come see me after class."

No folded sheet on a desk corner in the third row back, where I spotted a yellow satin polo shirt dozing.

"How'm I supposed to talk to you, you back there? What should I call you? Should I call you Ninety-four?"

"That's not my name m'sieur. My name is Bien-Aimé."

"Oh, good, because I said to myself, he didn't put his name at the corner of the desk because it's already written on his shirt."

"It don't mean that, m'sieur."

"So what is that, then, Ninety-four?"

"I dunno, it's some figure."

"You mean a number."

"That's right, a figure."

The bell had the effect of a firecracker in a drowsing henhouse. I watched from the corner of my eye as Mezut considered whether I had forgotten or not, then decided not to risk it and approached in silence, first laying his self-portrait beside my attendance book.

"You planning to be like that all year long?"

His lowered head hid some expression I couldn't make out.

"I'm listening. You going to be like that all year?"

"Like what?"

"Like that business of I keep turning around in my seat and I give a stupid smile when someone speaks to me."

"There was something I didn't understand."

"You going to be like that all year?"

"No."

"Because if you're like that all year it's going to be war and you'll lose. Either it's war and it will be a nightmare for you, or you do things right and it'll go well. Have a nice day."

Geraldine was filling her grading book with student names.

"You seen them yet, the 9-cs?

The question was addressed to Leopold, who was surfing on some Goth site and didn't turn around.

"Yep, for a minute."

"And?"

"Looked okay to me."

"Yeah, same here, but we'll see."

A masked Amazon in a leather bodysuit was inviting our internaut Leopold to come join her in the Underworld.

"What about you, you seen the 8-as?"

"For a minute."

"And?"

"Looked okay to me."

"Yeah, same here, but we'll see. Some teachers are already complaining about them."

Lina raised her voice over the copy machine, which was rapidly spitting forth a cartoon of Don Quixote. One sheet after another, all the same.

"I don't know if I'm allowed to screen a TV show for the kids?"

No one offered to clarify the juridical principle raised.

"I mean, because I'd like to show them *Hasta Luego*. It's a series on Channel Six."

Geraldine was scanning the 10-cs list, calculating the proportion of girls.

"We don't get Six at the house."

"It's a really good series."

"Not Six, and not One, either."

"It's a little silly, but that's just why the kids might like it."

"The other day my father-in-law was over for the weekend, he wanted to watch the news on Channel One, we told him sorry, can't get it."

Valerie blew in, angry.

"Goddam, it's just not tolerable, putting up with that. You see them yet, the 8-AS?"

"Yeah, for a minute."

"Because me, I think they're crazy nuts. One period, and I've already written up three incident slips."

Lina had stuck a bulky video player under her arm. "It's the 9-BS I'd like to do *Hasta Luego* with. Anybody seen them yet?"

"Yeah, for a minute."

"And?"

"They look okay."

"Same here, but we'll see."

Small sheet large-graph paper: My name is Souleyman. I am kind of quiet and shy at school. But outside I am a different person, excited-like. I do not go out much. Just to boxing. I would like to have success in life in air-conditioning after, and main thing I do not like conjugation.

Small large-graph looseleaf sheet: Khoumba is my name but I do not like it much. I like French class even if the teacher is no good. People say I am mean-tempered it's true but it depends if I get respect.

Sheet from scratchpad: Djibril is my name. I am Malian and I am proud because this year Mali will be playing in the Africa Cup. In the draw it came out they going to play Libi and Algeri and Mozambic. I like my school because the teachers they let you alone cep if you get too ressless. Too bad I will leave here at the end of the year because I am in ninth grade.

Large sheet small-graph paper: My name is Frida, I am fourteen years old and that is also the same number of years that I have been living in Paris with my father and my mother. I have no brother or sister but many friends. I like music, movies, theater and ballet which I have been doing for ten years. Later on I would like to be a lawyer because I think it's the best profession in the world and that it is great to defend people. Personality-wise, I am very nice and agreeable to be with, but my parents say I think too much. On the other hand sometimes I have moods and I think it is because I was born under the sign of Gemini.

Small large-graph sheet torn from spiral pad: My name is Dico and I have nothing to say about myself because nobody knows me except me.

Ruled sheet torn from appointment pad: My name is Sandra and I am a little bit sad to be coming back to school but also glad because I like school, especially French class and history class, when we learn about how human beings have made the world we live in today. I have lots more things to say but you are going to collect the papers soon because I was too worried about doing something good and I only began to write two minutes ago excuseme for the misteakes.

Small-graph sheet torn from spiral pad: Tony Parker is the best basketball player. That why he plays in america. He is little but he runs fast and he makes great 3 point shots. So really he is big. When he is next to a reporter it the reporter who is little. Signed: Mezut.

Small large-graph sheet, perforated edge: My name is Hinda, I am fourteen and I am glad to be alive. Later I would like to teach children. I would like to be in a nursery, that way it's less work, just a sheet of paper and a marker that keeps them busy all day long. No, I'm kidding, just I really like children and also books about love.

Small sheet large-graph: My name is Ming. I am fifteen years old, I am a Chinese. I live in 34 rue de Nantes 75019 with my parents and I going to school with my frens. My good points is I am nice and hard worker. My bad points is I am curious.

Half-sheet drawing tablet: My name is Alyssa, I am thirteen years old and have problems with my knee because I grew too fast. French class I don't know what I think about it yet. Sometimes I like it, and sometimes I think it is totally useless to wonder about questions that have no answers. I would like to be a humanitarian doctor because a humanitarian doctor told me about his work and I knew that that was what I should do. I will not say any more, I leave it to you to judge for yourself.

I strolled among the desks, casting an unseeing eye at the workbooks hidden by elbows as I passed. I was bored.

"All right let's see what we've got. Give me a phrase using 'after' plus a verb. Hadia what do you suggest?"

Black plastic earrings marked with pink hearts, LOS ANGELES 41 on her sweatshirt. "After he gone to school, he came home."

I wrote her dictation on the blackboard and stepped back. "All right, what's the problem here?"

A silent Hadia.

"Yesterday I told you that after 'after,' we use the indicative, not the subjunctive. Why? Because the subjunctive expresses only hypothetical things, actions that aren't certain. For instance— Mezut? If you'd kindly look this way."

"I don't understand the question, m'sieur."

"Start by listening to it, you'll find it's easier to answer. Cynthia?"

Pink stitching on a black T-shirt. "It is necessary that I go—um, necessary that I go to school."

"Very good, that's an example of the subjunctive, something's not sure. But when we say 'after' about an action, the action is certain—

it has already occurred, it's now 'afterwards'—so there we use the indicative. So in this other sentence, what do we do? Cynthia again."

"Umm . . . 'After he went . . . has gone . . . went to school, he returned home.'"

I wrote on the blackboard as she spoke. "Good, you used the indicative with 'after,' that's right. The only little problem is, and it's the second thing wrong with Hadia's example, is that actually we don't use the simple past tense there, we use the past participle, which is?"

"Umm—'After he has gone to the pool, he has went home.'"

"Yes, but no. You have to use the past participle right through the whole sentence."

"Umm—'After he has gone to the pool, he is gone home.'"

"Watch out for the auxiliary verb—'be' and 'have' are not interchangeable."

"Umm—'After he has went—'"

"No! Watch it!"

"Umm—"

"You had it."

"Umm—'After he has gone to the pool he has gone home.'"

"That's it."

Just then Alyssa sat straight up.

"But m'sieur, that's not always true, that the action is already over when we say 'after' something."

Damn.

"What do you mean?"

"Well, frinstance if I say 'You must . . . it is necessary that you . . . after you do . . . something'—I dunno, that means the person hasn't done the thing yet, so there you use the subjunctive usually."

"It's true that in that case we could use the subjunctive but actually not. In that case, we use a peculiar tense called the 'future anterior.' 'After you *will have* played the game, it *will be* necessary that you eat.'"

"That's not logical."

"You could say that, yes, but you know, that rule about 'after he such and such'—nobody really knows it and everybody makes the grammatical error, so it's not worth getting too worked up over it."

I had slept badly, they were all sleeping. The door opened without a knock and Sandra was there, and the walls shifted.

"Good morning."

It was a "good morning" with a more urgent purpose than apologizing for a late arrival, she was already on her way to the back of the room, sweeping past her usual place beside Hinda, who resembled I can't think who and was looking sad today, the sparkle dulled in her handsome dark eyes. Sandra threw her bag onto the table where Soumaya sat by herself in the last row and took a seat beneath the poster about Holidays in Ireland.

"How come you're changing your seat like that?"

"Because, m'sieur."

"Oh, I see, of course, now that you explain it you've convinced me."

"I can't tell you m'sieur."

"Some classified military secret?"

"What's that mean m'sieur?"

"Meaning it's a state secret?"

"What's 'state secret' mean m'sieur?"

"Meaning a very very secret secret."

"That's right."

They were supposed to have written an aphorism using the general truth present tense. Gibran was snickering behind his hand over something or other, echoing Arthur, who was snickering behind his hand over something or other.

"Gibran, I'm listening."

"What m'sieur?"

"I'm ready to hear your aphorism."

"My what, m'sieur?"

"Your aphorism."

"I dunno what it is, that thing m'sieur."

"It's what you were assigned to do for today."

Someone knocked and Mohammed Ali came in, TRENDY-89-PLAYGROUND.

"Did I say to come in?"

"No m'sieur."

"And you came in anyhow?"

"You want me to go back out m'sieur?"

"No no it's all right. You have a note?"

"Well no m'sieur, because I thought how like its no sense getting even later stopping at the office and all."

"And why are you late?"

"It's my elevator m'sieur."

"It's slow?"

"No m'sieur, it gets jammed all the time."

"That must have been awful."

"No, that's OK, it's chill."

Zineb's hand had been up for two minutes. Pink bandana knotted at the neck, plastic earrings, same color.

"Can I tell my aphorism?"

"Go ahead."

"I'm not sure it's any good."

"Go ahead."

"I warn you I'm not sure it's right."

"I'm listening."

"What doesn't kill you makes you stronger."

"Very good."

Mohammed Ali had just sat down, TRENDY 89 PLAYGROUND.

"Me m'sieur I don't agree. Frinstance you break both legs, well you're not dead but you're not as strong."

"It's better to just stay put in a jammed elevator, that way nothing happens."

Hinda raised her hand and her dull gaze.

"Yes?"

"Betraying a friend is like betraying yourself."

A cry of outrage, cracks in the walls, Sandra,

"You're a fine one to talk."

Soumaya echoed her.

"Just start with your own self, then we'll see."

Hinda, looking like I can't think who, did not deign to hear their invectives.

"Other examples?"

Sandra, under HOLIDAYS IN IRELAND.

"Respect others as you want them to respect you."

"Are you using the familiar address *tu* to me now?"

"No, it's in the aphorism."

"All right then."

As was fitting, Fangjie and Ming shared a desk. I had noticed their names on the class list without wondering about their level of spoken French. Now I was worried about calling on them and causing them to tense up with incomprehension like porcupines snared by a paw. During the first exercise I craned over their shoulders. Their written sentences were neither more nor less correct than other students', but this was a grammar class, and they might be transcribing the sentence mechanically from the lesson book.

When I reached their desk after circling through the room during the correction review it became necessary to get into it. Ming seemed less panicky. He read the sentence with a strong accent, stumbling over one tough verb but able to identify the tenses.

Toward the end of the hour he even volunteered to pick out the examples of verbs in the different tenses. He stopped at *etait tombé*. I chose not to point out that the participle "fallen" following the "had" makes "had" an auxiliary verb, not the verb itself, properly speaking; I was betting on the silence of the other students. No one spoke up right away, but I did not dare claim victory, because Frida had her hair pulled back and shrewd little eyes.

"M'sieur, 'had' isn't really the verb, it's the auxiliary. After it there's 'fallen,' so 'fall' is the verb, not 'have.'"

"Yes, but 'have' has to be conjugated even when it's an auxiliary, so it could be considered a verb."

"So then is 'fall' the verb here, or is it 'have'?"

"A little bit both."

"It's what you call a dilemma, except that in this case it's supertragic because either way you lose. On one side you've got life, existence, and existence is what?—sickness, suffering, the death of loved ones, lots of other stuff too, but still it's all those hard things you have to undergo. And on the other side, well—you've got death, nothing-ness—that is, for all the people who don't believe in God. So overall, either you suffer or you die, knowing that in the end you'll have to go through both. That's it, roughly speaking, that's the way it is, to be or not to be. To be suffering or not to be at all, that is, to die. Have I answered your question, Lydia?"

Mohammed spared her a polite lie.

"M'sieur, you rather be or not be?"

"That is the question."

"Me I rather be."

"You're right, but we'll go on with the lesson now."

By way of example of the present tense used as immediate future, I'd written, "Bill is leaving for Boston tomorrow." Djibril began to speak without asking permission, ADIDAS 3 in small letters beneath a triangular shield on the left side of his chest.

"Why is it always Bill or like that?"

"You raise your hand when you want to speak."

He did it.

"Why's it always Bill or like that? Why's it never, I dunno, Rashid or some other name?"

I was annoyed that my strategy for dodging the problem hadn't worked.

"If I start trying to represent every nationality with people's names I'll never get done with it. But okay, we'll say Rashid, just to make Djibril happy."

At the back of the room some unidentified voice muttered Rashid, that's a dumb name, but my hand had already erased BILL and was carefully shaping the letters of RASHID. Rashid is leaving for Boston tomorrow.

Gilles dropped a flat tablet into a glass of water. Struggling with the copying machine, Sylvie said,

"You look tired."

"Yeah, I dunno."

He hesitated to elaborate, foreseeing that to do so would depress him still more, then went ahead and elaborated anyhow.

"It's the eighth-graders. They're starting to give me . . ."

To finish the sentence, he pinched his Adam's apple twice between thumb and index finger. Leopold had a row of rings at the crest of each ear.

"Listen, if you saw the 7-AS!"

Elise agreed.

"They're nutcases, I swear! I already filled out four incident slips this morning. If this keeps up it's gonna be the end for me. Last year my blood pressure went crazy, I have no desire to start up with that again, thank you very much."

For the third time Marie scooped her useless coin from the base of the coffee machine. "Does anyone have change for fifty centimes?"

The effervescent tablet began dissolving in Gilles' glass.

"There are some dreadful kids in 8-D. Hadia for instance, she's unbearable."

Jean-Pierre smiled from the corner sofa. "You know what 'Hadia' means in Arabic? 'Silent nobility.'"

Gilles swallowed the now-bubbling liquid in one gulp. Bastien asked him if he wanted

". . . a cookie with that?"

"Wouldn't help."

Valerie had a picture magazine open on her lap, with Claude at her side craning over at it.

"I'm a Scorpio, means I'm pretty easy-going, you know, and at the same time also kind of moody."

"I'm a Gemini."

"Aiee! With what rising?"

"Leo rising."

"Oh, well yeah, you do have your little quirks."

"Why?"

"Usually that's how it is, Leo rising—those folks are touchy."

"Oh really? Watch it you Scorpio, just go easy there."

"Listen, Scorpios are straightforward, direct."

"Oh sure."

"So—you're Gemini?"

"Yeah . . ."

"To me, Geminis . . ."

"What about Geminis?"

"Well, Geminis, they're not real comfortable in their skin. They sort of, they chafe, you know, just not real natural."

"Pisces are the ones who chafe."

"No, I mean, Geminis are like double-faced, you know what I mean? No? Aren't you double-faced, yourself?"

"I sure am, I'm an English teacher by day and by night I'm a serial killer."

Not a twitch of the neck from anyone. The guidance counselor was explaining the study programs possible in high school after students finished ninth grade here. She studded her account with questions punctuated by anonymous and laconic responses from the audience that wrongly convinced her of their understanding, authorizing her to go on with the outline sketched on the blackboard.

"You have two major families of curriculum starting in high school—the vocational and the general academic or technological. Now: the vocational is called that why?"

"Because it's for working."

"Very good, that's right, it provides for quicker entry into the working world. You might say that what they teach there is closer to the area of skills-training."

Nobody asked the meaning of skills-training.

"So for instance, in the BEP secretarial course you'd learn to write a letter, whereas in the STT you'd do something more in the area of business law."

Nobody asked the meaning of business law. On the bent back of Djibil's jersey the letters DJIBIL made a half-circle above the impressive numeral 5. Dianka and Fortunée were chuckling at something outside the window. The others sat in listening posture.

"So now: At the end of ninth grade, you'll have to fill out an application for the high school you choose—that is, the high school you'll choose according to what's possible. For the choices, you see there's this chart with an abscissa and an ordinate—Down and Across—with the abscissa listing what you want to do and ordinate what you can do. Roughly speaking, you have to work out a compromise between wish and reality."

She wrote the two words on the blackboard with a slash between them.

"When you've worked out a good compromise, the principal of your middle school will register the class council choices, and then it'll be up to you to follow through with the next steps."

Nobody asked about "register." The guidance counselor distributed green slips to fill out on the spot. Wish/Reality. I moved from the back of the room to collect the slips from the rows. Huang had no idea where to start. Nervously, he began to fill out the questionnaire. Faced with "mother's profession" he wrote in "textile machinist."

"Out of twenty-four papers, only two show a rough understanding of the term 'meaning of life.' What does that mean, the meaning of life?"

Frida, LOVE ME TWO TIMES in black on a pink t-shirt.

"It means a what a person is here for."

"We raise our hand when we want to speak. Okay, what's a person here for?"

The four boys at the back were not listening.

"Kevin you have no interest in the meaning of life?"

"Wha?"

"We don't say 'wha.'"

"What did you say?"

"The meaning of life doesn't seem to interest you."

"Sure it does."

"So what is it?"

"*I* dunno."

"In that case, listen to the other people and you will know. Frida, can you tell us how we give meaning to life?"

Frida didn't have to search for the answer, she found it right off. "Like, I don't know, frinstance if a person believes in God and all."

"Fine, exactly. People who believe in God, that's a way of giving a meaning to existence. And people who don't believe, what do they do?"

The four at the back were not listening.

"Kevin, what do you say to people who think they might as well just shoot themselves?"

"I dunno."

"You let them go ahead?"

Lydia spoke up without raising her hand.

"The meaning is also helping other people."

"We raise our hands to talk. Help them how, Lydia?"

"Ahh, I dunno, like giving them food."

"Yes, that's right, good, for instance we can make ourselves useful by what we call humanitarian commitment, that sort of thing. And what else?"

She smiled. "Teaching them things."

"Teaching whom?"

"Other people."

"So then a teacher's life has meaning?"

"Well yeah, because he has like a mission and all."

"You mean he was put on earth for that reason?"

"Maybe . . . I dunno."

Sprawling in his chair in the left first row, Dico emerged from his silence.

"She just runnin her mouth. So m'sieur, already when you were born did you wanna be a teacher?"

"No. Not till I was two or three."

"Well yeah, at's what I mean, she just says whatever."

At the start of the individual help sessions I asked the students to read that day's assignments from their pads. Rather ugly Sofiane started reading the instructions for an art project. Her timid voice was barely audible, and it became clear that her assignments had been poorly noted, which was what I wanted to demonstrate. I had her repeat her recital, and she kept skipping over one of the terms. Testy because it was Monday, I brusquely snatched the pad from her. The muddled term, scribbled after "imagine a credible," was practically illegible. Youssuf, UNLIMITED 72, deciphered it as "scenario." I turned back to Sofiane.

"How come Youssuf wrote 'scenario' and you didn't?"

"I dunno."

"Still, 'scenario' is a word you know, isn't it?"

"No."

"Oh, you don't know the word? The rest of you people—you must know what 'scenario' means, certainly."

No one validated that certainty.

"Scenario? Really?"

Eventually Yelli moved hesitant lips.

"It's, like, the story kind of."

"Good. That's it, it's the story, not the pictures. Before a director starts making a movie, he has a kind of big book that tells what the characters do and what they say. So 'imagine a credible scenario' means what? What did your teacher want you to do?"

Even Yelli didn't budge. My feet dug into the platform.

"Credible—what does that mean?"

Mody would have loved to know, to raise his hand, and to say the answer. Lacking it, he threw out words at random. "Interesting? Wise? Serious?"

"Yes, that's right, it's a little like 'serious' but more particular. 'Credible' comes from the verb *croire*, to believe—it means a thing you can believe. For instance, if Mody came in late and told me he'd had to kill off a bunch of Martians that spurted up out of his sink, I'd tell him, 'Mody, your excuse is not credible.' On the other hand, if he told me that he woke up late, I still might not believe him, but I *could*—it would be possible to believe him, it's 'credible.' So 'Imagine a credible scenario'—now do you all understand that?"

A few heads sketched a 'yes' barely distinct from a 'no.'

"What you have to do is imagine a story, but not fall over into craziness, like for example 'Yesterday I woke up I had eight legs and I hid inside a mushroom to eat penguin ears in mayonnaise.' I really think your teacher must have been afraid of nonsense, that's all, and that's why she asked for something credible. So there you are, that's what you were supposed to do for today—but if you didn't understand what she said, how did you manage to do it?"

Still empty at the appointed hour, the study hall, rearranged specially for the event, slowly began to fill. People kept arriving to take seats around the U of tables after the principal, at the head of the U, had already opened the discussion.

"If everything goes according to the law, foreign newcomers will first go into an intensive French language class, then into an orientation class, and only then will they enter a regular middle school, with the option of doing a course in French as a Second Language or French as a Foreign Language."

Marie took an uncontested turn at speaking.

"Is there a structure available for the non-French-speaking pupils who aren't Chinese? I've got a case like that in sixth grade."

A scowl of concern distorted the principal's face.

"The problem is that there is so little room, we have to consider priorities. If you find ten students like that one, we could put them together a class. But until then, we have to work with the largest numbers, and—take a look at your geography—that's the Chinese."

Unmoved by the humorous parenthesis, Marie dove back into correcting papers. Claude had never been distracted from his. Alongside him Leopold, with three rings in each eyebrow, opened a file folder to reveal a poster page featuring a vamp with enormous wide eyes done up in greasepaint.

"Who's that?"

Leopold whispered some Italian name.

"What kind of music?"

"Metal."

"There *is* such a thing, Italian metal?"

"Oh yes, her group is one of the best in Europe."

The principal was still talking.

"What I propose is the following: that one member of each instruction group locate which day in the schedule the students risk having really heavy bookbags, and see what can be done to lighten them."

That interested Valerie, Claude, and Danièle.

"Oughta start by seeing to it they don't take home any more than they have to."

"They have to be taught to carry only what's needed."

"There should be a collection of textbooks available in the classrooms."

Leopold was looking over the words of a song he had copied out in gothic letters on the back of his folder.

"What does that say?"

"It's a suicide note."

"She killed herself?"

"Well of course not, since she's singing."

"Am I a dope."

The principal was still talking.

"The advantage of our point system is like the one for the driver's license: the student knows when there'll be a penalty and it's an incitement to slow down. The disadvantage is also the same as with the license: as long as he still has points left, he can go as fast as he likes with impunity. It may be necessary to invent a penalty system that has him lose all the points at once, but in that case we might as well not bother with points in the first place, so it's complicated."

He forced himself to raise the volume of his soft voice in order to be heard over the private conversations, which were becoming less and less so. With little conviction, he went on to raise a couple of further points of discussion, then suggested a pause before we broke into groups to lay the groundwork for a schoolwide plan. The proposal had the effect of a factory whistle in a henhouse: Silence first, then chairs shoved back by heavy legs that finally left the room.

In the bathroom, Jacqueline and Chantal were sharing the sink.

"Till what time will this go on, do you think?"

"Whatever, I've got my kids to pick up at school."

"Damn, out of towels."

I walked toward the end of the corridor. The custodians had deserted their station. I swiped a sugar packet and opened the doors to the metal cabinet looking for a dishtowel.

"It starts with the number one."

I turned to the door from which that mannered voice seemed to come, but the man was standing at the opposite side, against the light of the window flooded with sunshine. A shadow.

"Counting to a hundred starts with one. If the one is missing, the count is no good."

I had never heard that ageless voice.

"The one doesn't guarantee the hundred, but without the one, no hundred."

He pulled out a blue striped towel from the upper shelf of the cabinet and laid it against my torso. "One, two, three, four, five, six, seven, eight, nine, ten, eleven . . ."

Back in the study hall, the counting went on in my brain. Depopulated, the U awaited the first returnee from the break to draw others back. Taking her seat with a mug of hot chocolate in hand, twenty-one twenty-two twenty-three, Lina asked me with quiet sarcasm what a "schoolwide plan" was.

"We have to define broad goals and suggest ways to get to them."

Twenty-nine, thirty, back to counting drops, exaggerating the stupidity of the situation.

"What do we have to do?"

"What are we supposed to talk about?"

Thirty-four, thirty-five, sitting back down herself, Geraldine offered to keep minutes of the meeting. Rachel began the discussion.

"Well, I propose a project on uncivil behavior. They're endlessly throwing insults back and forth at each other, that should be punished in some systematic way."

"We should photocopy the Complete Roughneck Dictionary and make them translate from it each time."

"What's that?"

"It's this book that lists slang expressions from the projects and gives you the equivalent. For instance, '*faquin*' is 'bastard.'"

Claude neither laughed nor raised it one better, facing into the general tendency to do so like a headwind.

"The main problem, we all agree, is the seventh graders. They're the ones we have to do something about."

Gilles spoke up for the first time all afternoon.

"I'm sorry but we're paying for last year's stupid mistakes. Last year in the sixth grade they were already making serious trouble, a couple of discipline committee hearings would have quieted them down."

Bastien hastily swallowed his cookie and spoke without asking permission of Geraldine, who was in charge of granting it.

"And besides, it's typical trash behavior, they're constantly challenging you."

Valerie spoke without asking permission of Geraldine, who was in charge of granting it.

"Still, you realize that the kids who are pulling this crap don't understand anything, what's needed is to take them aside and start everything over again from zero."

One, two, Gilles suddenly doubled his usual number of comments.

"I'm sorry but among the bad kids there are lots who are not poor students at all."

"Yeah, but the others no."

To conclude this day of reflection, the principal broke out champagne. By now we were only a dozen, thirteen, fourteen, fifteen. Correctly popped, the cork from the first bottle bounced against the wall, then rolled to rest beneath a desk.

Dianka was laughing over something or other with Fortunée, her knee showing above the desk and LIFESTYLE across her vest. She played deaf the first time I called her name. I raised my voice. "Sit up straight."

She did it halfheartedly.

"Better than that."

She stiffened ironically.

"All right, I'm listening."

"Wha?"

"I'm listening, I said."

She wavered about still pretending not to understand. Every second was a brick walling her into her game. Her neighbor murmured something that made her smile.

"OK, you come see me after class. Amar, sentence five, I'm listening."

"Camels drink little water."

"Now, why is that in the present tense?"

"General truth."

"Yes, it's a general truth, something that can't be contested."

Khoumba, red beads at the tips of her braids, did not raise her hand.

"M'sieur some camels do drink."

"Yes, but very little."

"More than people."

"Only proportionally."

"So it's not a general truth."

"Yes it is."

"You said if anyone disagrees then it's not a general truth, well I disagree."

The bell had the effect of a breadcrumb tossed into a pigeon coop. Out of the corner of my eye I watched Dianka wondering whether I'd forgotten or not. She came up, casting a glance at Fortunée, who would be waiting for her in the hallway. LIFESTYLE.

"Hand me your home-note booklet and look at me."

She resisted only half the command. I looked for the page meant for notes to the parents.

"You're to write out ten good resolutions for the year. Get it signed at home. I'm adding that if you persist in your attitude I'll ask for a three-day suspension. Look at me when I talk to you."

She and her chum were communicating by eye. I'd slept badly.

"You're an imbecile, it's amazing what an imbecile you are."

"You can't go insulting me no way."

"It's not an insult, it's the truth, if I say you're an imbecile it's because you are an imbecile, if I say you're an idiot it's because you're an idiot, if I say you're stupid it's because you're stupid. And the day you are no longer an imbecile, an idiot, or stupid, I will say: 'Dianka is intelligent, clever, and . . . intelligent.'"

"You're not spose to talk to me like that."

"I'll insult you if I want, if I feel like saying you're an imbecile I'll say you're an imbecile, and if I do say it it's because it's true, you *are* an imbecile, I've got three classes and right now you're the one—by a big margin—who holds the title of the champion imbecile student. By a very big margin."

"Fine."

"No it's not fine. Three months from now you'll be saying to yourself god why was I so stupid, you'll be saying why did I waste my time with my stupid tricks, three months from now you'll be saying to yourself the French teacher was right, I should have listened to him, I would have started right up with the work and I wouldn't have wasted three months, that's what you'll be saying to yourself in three months, you wanna bet? You'll be saying I've been a jerk and I wasted my own time, so look, what I suggest is, tell yourself all that starting right now, that way there won't be any more problem. You can go now I've seen enough of you for today."

The passage in the novel described a rigid bourgeois woman.

"Does anyone know the meaning of 'drawn together with four pins'?"

From the ranks burst a bunch of anarchic and impermissible suggestions. I was glad of the chance to explain.

"The expression means when a lady is dressed very correctly, so neat that you might say she's held together by four pins or tacks pulling at her—you see what I mean?"

They saw, barely.

"It's actually the stiffness that matters most, you know those people who dress so carefully, always holding themselves tight so they don't mess anything up?"

Every word was a step backward.

"It's like the saleswomen at the Galeries Lafayette. You know the place, the Galeries Lafayette?"

Their silence and my powerlessness pushed me to take a sharp tone.

"No, of course you don't know it, since it's in a different *arrondissement* from this one."

Sandra, who had been only half-listening, sat up abruptly, knocking an elbow against the wall and hurting the wall.

"Look, all right, we're not peasants, the Galeries Lafayette, I go there almost every week so all right."

The bell interrupted her protests at the same time as the four-o'clock uproar, which tripled then evaporated in the corridors like a flight of ducks into the distance. I suddenly saw wild geese follow the ducks over the pond. They were heading toward the Midi, the Mediterranean. A flight of partridges rose over the lake and into the . . . Sandra mounted siege to my desk, flanked by Imani and Hinda, who looked like somebody, I can't think who.

"M'sieur, why're you always riding us like we don't know anything?"

"Not always, you're exaggerating."

"Yeah well with the Galeries Lafayette you got us real mad because, like, me I know it very well I go there every week."

"It's true that I sometimes get the feeling you never leave the neighborhood."

"Well that's wrong too m'sieur. My boyfriend he's in the seventeenth."

Airforce in to support artillery: Hinda stepped up. "That's not just some story m'sieur, her boyfriend is in the seventeenth, that's why she goes there all the time."

All I could do was retreat or set up a diversionary operation.

"So, the two of you have made up?

Sandra moved her big belt up over her little pot belly.

"That's our business, m'sieur."

Rain had begun to beat at the windowpanes. Sylvie was recording notes in the ad hoc ledger and Geraldine was bit by bit eroding a brioche set in the middle of the oval table.

"Actually, I'm looking more in the twelfth."

"That's true, the twelfth is nice."

"Yeah, there's some parts that really are nice."

"Not all, you gotta admit."

"No, not all."

"Come to that, the eleventh is good, because all of it is nice."
Lips pursed dubiously, Sylvie drew a long breath through her nose.
"All nice, I don't know about that. We'll have to see."
"Sure, it's not the sixth, no, but still, it's nice overall."
"Even the sixth isn't nice overall."
"Exactly, you know what I'm saying, the eleventh is lively everywhere, and it's mostly young folks, too."
"Not necessarily."
"Well, young, I don't know, but socially, you know, you don't run into these old super-rich bourjie ladies staring at you in the elevator, with their dogs and all."
Sylvie closed up her record book and picked off a bit of brioche with two fingers.
"Yes, but it's nice to live around teachers."

They filled the classroom with an afternoon hubbub. I asked everyone to sit down without success. Dico and Khoumba were swearing at each other in the back. I thought it was just the usual provocation routine, but the pitch rose and Dico shoved her. I rushed over to intervene. He fully expected to go on, but without actual violence.
"Go to your desk and sit down."
Khoumba irritated him by challenging him.

"You too, Khoumba, quiet down and go sit."

Futile orders. Drawn by the noise, younger kids had stopped on the threshold of the still open doorway. As I approached, they took off up to the next landing. Hélé, the one bringing up the rear, turned around.

"Come over here."

"What? S'not me."

"What do you mean, it's not you?"

"S'not me.

"Apologize."

"Excuse me."

"Good."

Dico and Khoumba were not backing down from their high, overplayed or not. I pressed Dico's arm to urge him toward his seat.

"Where you come off touching me?"

"Sit down."

"I'll sit down but you don't touch me."

Kevin was standing around in the aisle.

"What are you doing here?"

I was shouting. He pointed to the chair nearby.

"That's my seat."

"No that's not your seat there, you go to the rear." I pushed his back and he resisted by nothing but his near-obese bulk. I grabbed roughly at the straps of his backpack and it fell onto a single desk that was wedged into a corner.

"Why you mad at me?"

"I'll be mad at whoever I want. Who's the teacher, you or me?"

"M'sieur, you see this thing here he threw?"

Khoumba was waving the incriminating evidence, a ball of paper. Dico indicted himself by denying it before he was accused.

"Wasn't me I'm telling you! I don't give a fuck about her!"

"You don't give what?"

"I don't care about her."

"That's better."

I would have liked each student to come to the board to read his or her composition on pollution, but the Chinese girls couldn't do that. Jie maybe, Jiajia just possibly, but Liquiao and Xiawen would only mutilate a few phrases already full of holes. They were hoping I wouldn't put them through such an ordeal, and I was hoping the others wouldn't notice or would act as if they didn't. Halfway through the presentations I quit requiring them to come to the board, but I asked for volunteers. Then I put an end to the exercise by saying that time was short. Mariama, diamond plug in left nostril, made her coarse voice heard.

"Why aren't they going up, Jie's gang?"

I lowered my head for a moment too long, then raised it without knowing what I was going to say.

"That's not a very nice way of expressing yourself."

"But why aren't they going up?"

"The people who want to do it come up, that's all."

"Just before though you told Frida to come up, and she didn't want to."

"That's because I was sure that what Frida had prepared was good."

"And them other kids who didn't go up—what they did is no good?"

"Can I go on with my lesson?"

In a show of disapproval, she sucked her tongue hard against her palate. It made a Pfffh sound.

"Is this a story where the characters are mice?"

Sandra asked the question without looking up from her assignment pad, where she was noting down the title of the book to buy.

"No, they're real people. There's just a story about mice for a short passage, you'll see."

"Sounds stupid."

"That's why I'm having you read it."

Mohammed Ali asked what auxiliary verb goes with *ému*. I asked what was the connection, there was none, I gave him the verb and asked if he could conjugate it. He started mumbling some M sounds and trying to stick some stubborn vowels onto them to make a word.

"*Émouvoir* is a word that was invented just to bug people. Even grownups have trouble with it, just try it on them, you'll see it's a disaster. Only the most cultivated people like me know what to do with it."

Mocking laughter drowned the room, punctuated with a few sardonic throat-clearings. Annoyed, I closed off my purposely comical parenthesis by putting my sentence on the board with a Jesuit-style austerity. When I turned back, Katia was babbling with her neighbor Imani.

"Katia!"

"What?"

"You know very well what."

"I'm not doing anything."

"Come see me after class."

"M'sieur that's not right, you're pissed off and you're taking it out on me that's not right."

"First off, you don't say 'pissed off,' you use a real French word, that will help."

"You're mad and you're taking it out on me that's not right m'sieur."

"It's not up to you to say if I'm mad or not, and now you be quiet unless you want things to turn out badly."

Imani raised her hand.

"M'sieur, it's true she wasn't talking, I was the one talking I swear."

"You want the punishment for yourself, is that it?"

"No m'sieur but Katia wasn't talking."

"Is Katia three years old? She can't defend herself?"

"Ah, m'sieur, really you hassle us too much."

"Can I go on with my class?"

"I swear you ride us too much."

"You can conjugate '*émouvoir*' in the *passé composé* if you insist on mouthing off."

I asked Khoumba to read the excerpt, and she said she didn't feel like it.

"Feel like it or not, read it."

"You're not gonna force me to read."

I turned to the twenty-four others for witness.

"What's that called, what Khoumba just did?"

"Insolence."

"Good, Kevin. It's good to have the word of an expert here."

Khoumba set about swallowing her syllables, as she always did when she objected, with a sidelong laugh because her pals around her were snickering. Lacking an idea for the moment, I told her to stay after class.

"Frida you were in the middle of explaining the word 'pervert' to us."

I LOVE UNGARO, said her sweatshirt.

"I don't know if it's right."

"Go ahead."

"Like it's a person who has strange ideas I dunno."

"For instance, if I want to eat the Eiffel Tower, am I a pervert?"

"No, not that kinda strange ideas, I dunno."

The bell sent the down feathers flying. Out of the corner of my eye I watched Khoumba take three authoritative steps forward to set her home-note booklet on my desk, NIKE ATLANTIC on her fake leather jacket, mouth clamped shut hard as if in fear someone would go searching for secret microfilm inside. I wrote out the particulars of her penalty together with a word for her parents: Write a hundred-line essay on an adolescent learning respect, to be turned in signed by parents the day after tomorrow. Before handing her back the booklet, I wanted to get a handle on my temper.

"Is it going to be like this all year?"

"All year what?"

"Apologize."

"For what? I didn't do anything."

"Apologize. Until you apologize I'm not letting you leave."

She hesitated between saving face or rejoining her pals, who were taking turns sticking half a head into the doorway.

"Fine, I got nothing to apologize for I didn't do anything."

To annoy me she made a move to snatch the away the booklet I was holding in the air to annoy her.

"Oh no you don't. Pull my arm off while you're at it."

She closed off again.

"What happened this summer—did you find out something unpleasant about me?"

On the surly offensive.

"Why'd you say that?"

"I don't know. Last year we were pals, you liked me fine, and this year you make my life hell, so I figure maybe over the summer somebody told you bad stuff about me."

"My mother's waiting for me."

"She's waiting for you to apologize."

"Sorry."

"Sorry what?"

"Sorry that's all."

"Sorry what?"

"I dunno."

"Repeat after me: Monsieur I'm sorry for being insolent to you."

"I wasn't insolent."

"I'm waiting: M'sieur I'm sorry for being insolent to you."

"M'sieur-I-am-sorry-for-being-insolent-to-you."

It was recited mechanically, with a pointed absence of conviction. Still, I handed over the booklet, which she seized quickly before skipping toward the door. As she disappeared into the corridor she cried, "I didn't mean it."

I bounded after her but too late. Her little rebel silhouette tore down a flight of stairs. I gave up, yelling threats after her. Returning to my desk, I kicked over a chair. Four hooves in the air.

1. What are the values of the school in a republic, and what should be done to bring society to recognize them? **2.** What should be the missions of a school in the Europe era and through the decades to come? **3.** Toward what sort of equality should a school move? **4.** Should education be divided differently as between youth and adulthood, and more thoroughly involve the working world? **5.** What common foundation of knowledge, skills, and standards of behavior should students master as a matter of priority by the end of each stage of the mandatory schooling? **6.** How should the school adapt to the diversity of the students? **7.** How can we improve recognition for, and the organization of, the vocational track? **8.** How can students be motivated and brought to work effectively? **9.** What should be the functions of and the modalities for evaluating students, for grading, and for examinations? **10.** How should student guidance be organized and improved? **11.** How should we prepare and organize the move into higher education? **12.** How can parents and other external partners of the school foster the students' academic success? **13.** How can we take care of those students in serious difficulty? **14.** How should handicapped or gravely ill students be schooled? **15.** How shall we battle effectively against violence and uncivil behavior? **16.** What should be the relations among the members of the educational community, in particular between parents and teachers, and between teachers and students? **17.** How can the quality of life of students in school be improved? **18.** In matters of education, define and assign the respective roles and responsibilities of the State and the regional or local communities. **19.** Should schools be granted greater autonomy, and should this be accompanied by evaluation? **20.** How can the school best use its available means? **21.** Should the school's practices be redefined? **22.** How should instructors be trained, recruited, and evaluated, and how can their careers be better organized?

Beneath the globe where the USSR reigned in red, Mohammed and Kevin were battling over the seat beside Fouad. In the end the former decided to oust Bamoussa, who protested that he always sat there for French class.

"If you want his seat, Mohammed, find a better argument than that."

"All he has to do is get out."

"That's not an argument."

"If Bamoussa stays there, there'll be too much pollution in the room, and that's bad for the ozone layer."

"That's better. But you don't show us in what way he pollutes."

"With his burnt-up sneakers, he pollutes."

"Your sneaks burned up, Bamoussa?"

"He's the one burnt 'em."

Souleyman, already sitting, had his hood pulled forward.

"Hood, Souleyman, if you please."

He sent it sliding onto his shoulders with a backward toss of his head, uncovering his shaved scalp. Fortunée wore glasses now and didn't make a fuss. Khoumba had LOVE spelled three times in a column on her pullover and was unpacking her things without the least intention of handing in what she owed me. I bent over her desk.

"Give me your booklet."

"Why?"

"You know very well why."

In her penalty assignment I replaced the hundred lines by a hundred and fifty.

"The next time you'll think first about what you say. And acually you're lucky, you've got two weeks to do your penalty."

"I'm not gonna do it anyway."

I turned on my heel to keep myself from insulting her. Fury. As I walked back to the platform, she mumbled something that made her seatmate laugh. Worse fury. Dounia to starboard.

"M'sieur, on the television they were saying there's gonna be a debate in the middle schools?"

"Just get out your folder."

Amar to port.

"You gonna give us homework over vacation?"

"Would you like that?"

"Yes."

"Then I won't give any."

Lina left off blowing on her tea to note my busy scissors.

"Good lord you never stop working, you."

Without remarking on my lack of reply, she addressed Geraldine, who was distractedly scanning the official document on the national schools debate tacked up on the corkboard.

"Don't be so low, Gégé."

"I'm not low at all, I'm finished tonight."

"That's right, you have no classes Friday."

Running through like a gust of wind, Luc sent my pile of exercise papers flying and said,

"—these privileges, it's really infuriating."

Lina cut short a swallow.

"You can't complain, you work only Friday mornings. Look at me—excuse me but I don't get out until five o'clock."

"Yes but I do still have four hours in a row, if you don't mind."

"Please, morning hours, that's nothing."

"Yeah but four in a row, thank you very much."

With shadows under his eyes that stretched out to his ears, Gilles was fingering a cigarette and yearning for a smoking room.

"Depends on the students. If it's the eighth graders, it's worse."

Standing beneath the woman with the parasol, three rings in each of his ears, Leopold disagreed.

"Well the seventh graders, I don't even want to tell you. I put in two incident reports again yesterday. With them, it's not even worth the trouble on Fridays. Morning or not."

Rachel had just jammed the photocopy machine.

"Why doesn't this do both sides, this piece of shit?"

Gilles didn't let go.

"The eighth graders, they're the pits."

"You do look tired, really."

"Yeah, I don't know . . ."

"You'll be able to rest pretty soon, y'know."

"Yeah, maybe. Vacations stress me out."

twenty-eight

Coming up out of the metro, I stopped at the brasserie. A fifty-year-old guy was smoking without his hands, which were enlisted to hold his paper, on which a rugby player in white lifted his victorious arms. The uniformed waiter set a cup on the copper bar.

"Real good those Brits."

"They invented the game, what can I say."

Outside, the still-timid daylight revealed the Chinese butchers unloading a refrigerator truck. Past the corner, Serge the dean and Ali the monitor were assessing the sabotage to the bell system.

"Gotta get it fixed, what else can I say? Hey, hello, how you doing?"

"Super."

I didn't need to push open the massive wooden door. A cleaning woman was wiping her wet mop over the tile floor of the playing court. Wielding a straw broom, another woman piled leaves against the back wall of the inner courtyard. Behind the blue door shadowy-eyed Gilles, a bandage on his finger, was photocopying a textbook page. He raised his voice to be heard over the machine.

"Totally kills me to come back here."

"What's that?"

"I was building something and bang with the hammer."

Leopold pushed through the door next, and on his sweatshirt a vampire decreed APOCALYPSE NOW in English.

"Hey. What's that?"

"I was building something and bang with the hammer."

Valerie was checking her e-mails.

"Something else bothering you?"

"Doesn't it kill you to come back here? Me, totally."

Dico hung back from starting up the stairs after the others.

"M'sieur could I still change class?"

"It's more the class that would like to change Dico."

"A student can change head teacher?"

"Get going."

Most of the troop was waiting in front of the physics room. Frida was pouring out a story and a semi-circle of girls were drinking it up.

"So I go I'm not your ho, so he goes—"

"OK, into the room."

I'd slept badly. Mohammed pushed Kevin, who, exaggerating his loss of balance, bumped against the first desk to the left as he entered.

"M'sieur you see how he shoved me?"

"I don't care."

Dianka caught up to me at my desk.

"M'sieur, that book I couldn't find it."

"What book?"

"The one you told us to buy, with the mice in it."

"Everyone else found it, why not you?"

Souleyman had come into the room with his hood pulled forward. I waited till he sat down.

"The hood, Souleyman, if you please."

He slid it back onto his shoulders with a toss of his head.

"The cap too."

He lifted it off by passing his hand across the front of it, as if it were a balaclava. Dounia was looking at herself in the cover of her metal pencil kit. Dianka had not moved away.

"So it's no problem m'sieur if I don't have the book?"

"No, no. You'll just be putting yourself even more out to lunch than usual."

She turned away, pleased at not having to buy anything, and nearly tripped Fortunée, who wasn't wearing her glasses and was coming to hand me Khoumba's penalty paper. I held her off by raising the palm of my hand.

"Tell her to bring it to me herself."

So informed by her friend, Khoumba came forward from the back of the classrom with the sheet and wordlessly dropped it onto my desk.

An adolescent learns gradually to respect her teachers because of threats from them or because of fear of getting into trouble. These are just examples. And I respect you already and respect should be mutual. For instance I never tell you that you are hysterical so why do you tell me that? I have always respected you so I do not understand why you make me write this whole thing!! In any case, I know that you have some grudge against me but I do not know what I have done. I do not come to school to have my teacher give me a hard time for some unknown reasons! Would I do your job? NO!! I am your student and you are my teacher. So I do not see why you give me a hard time. You are supposed to enrich our knowledge of French. My resolution is to apply myself to all the schoolwork that way there will not be any more conflicts "for nothing" except if you "get after me." I admit I am insolent SOMETIMES but if people don't cause me to be I am not. All right, I return to the topic. When I say "because of threats from teachers" it's like where for example you wrote in my home-note booklet "I will have to take more serious measures" well that there's a threat (according to me!). And when I say "fear of getting into trouble" it means that the person is afraid of being sent to the principal's office or being expelled. In any case I promise to respect you if it is RECIP-ROCAL. Anyhow, I will not even look at you so you won't say that I am looking at you insolently. And usually in a French class, people should be talking about

French and not about their grandmother or their sister. So from now on I will not be talking to you.

I had discussed "victimism," and Mohammed Ali said that Arabs were always complaining about being victims of racism but they were just as racist as everyone else, and some people were even worse, like the people from Martinique, they thought they were more French than the Arabs, and Faiza said that the Martiniquais thought they were more French than the Malians but okay that's nonsense, and I said it is wrong to generalize, and at the bell Chen pulled away from the flying sparrow flock to head over to my desk, unconcerned about my lips, which I discovered an hour later were smeared with ink.

"M'sieur the problem is human nature, people will always want to destroy what's different from them, that's all, that's just how it is, that's fate."

With his lovely voice like an actor's dubbing for an adolescent in a movie, grinning with shyness at the audacity of his remark, he said,

"The thing we need is a common enemy, that way everybody would get together. Just pick out someone and problem solved."

Hakim tugged him toward the door by the strap of his backpack like he was forcing a lunatic back into the asylum.

"And besides that would solve the overpopulation thing, because the problem is there's too many people."

"In that case, Chen, it makes sense to pick the most numerous group for the enemy. Take a look at your geography book—who would that be?"

Dragged off by Hakim, he was backing away.

"Well, yeah—the Chinese."

"M'sieur, will we be doing dictations?"

"How is that connected with studying argumentation, Tarek?"

There was no connection. I picked up where I'd left off.

"So, give me an example?"

Everyone knew, but worried about not being able to explain. As an example of an example I chalked up a sentence saturated with specifics:

> On a winter evening at 5:30, a worker in his fifties walking on the rue du Faubourg Saint-Antoine ran across a surgeon's wife named Jacqueline.

The point was to illustrate a thesis—that the probability of unexpected encounters was greater in cities than in the countryside. They set to copying it down without understanding my intent.

"From the thesis to the example, we go from the particular to the general."

Hunched over her paper, Alyssa sat up like a question mark.

"Why sometimes they say 'particulars' for 'people'?"

"When does that happen?"

"Oh, like sometimes on television they say, I dunno, they're going to visit someone, they say *chez des particuliers*."

"Oh my, that has nothing to do with this. That's a different story."

Her question lived on in the grip of her teeth on the end of her pencil.

Djibril had begun to copy the line, and he looked up from his sheet, GHETTO STAR in green on his white sweatshirt.

"M'sieur, what's that name in the sentence?

"Jacqueline."

"That's too weird."

"It's 'Jacques' for a woman—the feminine form."

"Can we change it?"

"Put whatever you want."

He dove back into his note-taking.

"What are you going to put?"

"John."

"Well but John for the surgeon's wife—that won't work."

His brow furrowed.

"What about 'Jane'—is that a name?"

"Yes, sure."

On a winter evening at 5:30, a worker in his fifties walking on the rue Faubourg Saint-Antoine ran across a surgeon's wife named Jane.

"Did it ring?"

As she asked the question, Elise knew perfectly well that it had. Irene knew it too, especially since she had no class the next period.

"I don't care, I have no class next period."

Sitting beneath the painted blue waterlilies, Jacqueline and Geraldine were in agreement.

"It didn't work out well at all with the 7-AS. Yesterday I wrote two incident slips and threw one kid out of the room."

"Ten days of vacation isn't going to calm them down."

"Ten Discipline Councils is more like it."

"And then Ramadan—that tops it off."

Luc had left an incident slip in my locker:

ACCOUNT OF INFRACTION

Attention: Head Teacher.

At soccer, Dianka was insolent twice in a row. She hissed* the instructor as he was running with his students and made a scene when the teacher asked her to apologize. (*This is making a raucous sound out of the corner of the mouth; it means "go F__ yourself.")

Penalty: 2 hours detention at the school, Wednesday 8:35 to 10:25.

Copy out Physical Education rules from page 48 of the home-note booklet.

I had just finished reading the slip when its author turned up in a nylon parka. I'd had a bad night's sleep.

"You're sure that when they make that sound it means go fuck yourself?"

"What do you think? You think it means 'go have some fun in the hammam'?"

"All right."

He was already off.

"I cannot stand that sound."

"Pfffh."

"Stop, I can't stand it."

"Pfffh."

"You want two hours' detention?"

"Go have some fun in the hammam."

Souleyman came into the classroom with his hood pulled forward. I waited till he sat down to call it to his attention.

"The hood, Souleyman, if you would. And the cap, too."

He slid it back with a toss of the head, and took off the cap by sliding his hand across the front as you would do with a balaclava. I looked outdoors without seeing the trees, then my eyes came back to him.

"Souleyman, here's what I want you to do: for Monday— write me twenty lines that will convince me that it's very important for you to keep all that material on your head. If you do convince me,

I'll leave you alone about it till the end of the year. Shall we do that?"

He smiled, nodding his naked head. Waving Luc's report, I called out to Dianka as she went by my desk.

"You know what this is?"

"Well sure."

"Why did M'sieur Martin give it to me?"

"Because."

"Because what?"

"Because you're the head teacher."

"Because I'm the head teacher and I particularly asked the whole team of teachers to tell me everything that concerned you."

"Why?"

"Because."

She made the sound.

"It's funny you'd make that noise, beause that's just the thing you're in trouble for."

"I didn't do that in phys ed."

"So M'sieur Martin's lying?"

"I dunno. Just I didn't do it in phys ed."

"Well, I don't believe you didn't do it in phys ed, and you know why? Because you do it all the time, everywhere. Even though it makes everyone angry. True or false, that you do it everywhere?"

She lowered her head and her voice.

"Not everywhere."

"Yes, everywhere. You can go sit down."

She moved down the aisle. Pfffh.

The parent representatives sat on one side of the U, the teachers on another, and a third side fell to other staff members and to Sandra and Soumaya, who each set a Coca-Cola can in front of them as they took their seats. I didn't know they'd been elected student reps to the Administrative Council.

As Marie opened the session on amending the regulation on wearing political and religious markers in school, Sandra raised her hand and asked the exact meaning of "proselytizing." From four or five mouths stiff with solemnity, four or five definitions emerged, all speaking of negative effects on tolerance, respect, common values, the Republic. In view of that polyphony, the principal suggested postponing the vote to the end of the meeting, and taking up the day's second point of order.

"I'd like to submit to you the plan for changing schedules for the next year, for instance, starting classes at 8:15 instead of 8:25. That would allow a longer span of worktime over the day, and thus facilitate the distribution of activities."

A student's mother had already studied the file.

"The problem is, many of our students drop off their little brother or sister at the primary school on *rue* Debussy, and that also starts at 8:15. So they would have to drop them off a bit earlier, and the parents worry about leaving the little ones on their own, even for two or three minutes."

Sandra had pulled another can of Coke from her AMERICAN DREAM satchel, and she held it under the table to open it discreetly. It went *pschitt*, but the principal paid no attention, busy as he was with laying out the problems.

"Is it our job to worry about how the little children get to school? That's the question. And more generally, should we give our backing to families who hand off that responsibility to their older children? It's complicated."

A collegial groan from the parents.

"Some families can't take their children to school because they start work much earlier. It may not be our job to make up for problems in the school system, but it would be wrong not to do it knowing that it's that or nothing."

The two girls suddenly guffawed, at first letting it seem that their outburst had to do with the preceding remark, which was not the case. People waited for the thing to pass, going on with the discussions as if nothing were up. But it stretched on, grew worse, now the girls had collapsed onto the table, straining to smother their laughter, apologizing all the while. Feeble jokes began to spread along the U of tables to make up for the impossibility of clamping down in this democratic context. There was no longer any doubt that the girls were faking, trying to legitimize their laughter on the pretext that it was beyond control. After three heavily awkward minutes, they finally darted to the door, clutching their stomachs as if to keep from vomiting. Marie tried to draw attention back to the compromise she was laboring to put together.

"Couldn't we ask the primary school to start at ten after eight?"

Doubtful expressions from the parents.

"At that rate, everyone'll end up starting at five in the morning."

A facetious glint from the principal's face.

"The best thing would be to start at five in the afternoon, that way everyone would already be in place."

As we began to gather near the plastic goblets set out on a table covered with a paper cloth, the girls reappeared. They tossed their empty Coke cans into the plastic wastebasket and stationed themselves at the buffet, bold and timid at once, the one proportional to the other. The principal seized a bottle of the champagne provided by the school and pointed it toward the vase used for a balloting urn that stood in the center of the U of tables.

"How much do you bet?"

We watched his thumb nudge the cork out of the bottle; bursting forth with a cannon's report, it ended its curving flight at the foot of the chair that held the urn.

"Not so far off."

Some people voiced heavily obsequious compliments as they allowed their glasses to be filled. Small swarms gathered together by random shuffling about. Luc asked the two girls who Hinda's boyfriend was. Sandra took a handful of peanuts and in an old-lady voice parodied academic language:

"That, monsieur, we find ourselves constrained from revealing."

"Come to think, it's Ramadan today—are you sure you're allowed to eat?"

"Oh yes, it's past nightfall."

As I moved on with some remark and began to talk with Luc, Sandra nudged Soumaya, who whispered something to her, and the two left the circle to laugh. I pretended unconcern, but from the corner of my eye I saw them mimicking me, pinching their lower lips between thumb and forefinger.

I enunciated my questions, separating the words, and the students shaped their replies to match.

"Why the 'mice' in the title? Why-the-mice-in-the-title?"

Mezut hadn't read the book, but he copied the questions with great care and left blanks for answers that might land there like babies dropped by a stork. I had demanded absolute silence and also that no one should look at his neighbor's sheet. The reading quiz allowed for no conversation whatever.

"Reading quiz means zero talk. Same as with a dictation."

Tarek raised his Pavlovian hand.

"Yes, Tarek, there will be dictations. Fifty of them. But for the time being, we're doing a quiz and we have silence."

Everyone held to it except for Fangjie, who copied from Ming or asked the meaning of a word in the question, twisting her mouth to the side. Ming twisted his mouth in the opposite direction, straining between that task and the task of understanding me.

"Question nine, why doesn't the black groom sleep with the other people? Why-does-n't-the-black-groom-sleep-with-the-oth-er-peo-ple?"

Ming knit his brows like a blind man concentrating to identify a sound. I silently reread the sentence and realized that he was struggling with the word "groom." On the pretext that the word was unusual, I wrote it out on the board. Bien-Aimé uttered a cry of revolt.

"*Wesh*, how come before when I ask about a word you woulden write it and now you writing one?"

Caught red-handed.

"Because this is a hard word."

"No, me it's okay I know how to write it. Pfffh."

I looked down at my paper.

"And you know what it means, I suppose?"

His shoulders said Of course I know.

"Explain."

"It's a person who works at the stables."

Ming had understood and was writing the answer, meanwhile whispering it to Fangjie.

While I talked to a silent, inattentive class, while Gibran and Arthur were absorbed in a comparative analysis of their calculators and laughing at something or other, while Michael nodded Yes with his mind on other matters, while the walls drooped and would eventually cave in on us, Sandra burst into shameless laughter. I ordered her to quiet down, she signaled her incapacity to do so, still doubled over. I set my fists on my hips.

"That's not going to start up again like the other day."

She froze slightly in her squirming. I went on:

"I haven't had a chance to tell you this but frankly I was ashamed of you. You don't start laughing like that in a meeting of the Administrative Council, people were annoyed they couldn't stop you."

"Well so what? We left the room, didn't we?"

"After ten minutes of that, and it was ten minutes too much."

"Come on, it didn't bother anybody."

"Oh it certainly did. In fact people were very bothered, they didn't know how to tell you politely to stop it."

The onlookers were exchanging puzzled looks around the room. Soumaya was getting ready for a sulk. I went on emptying my knapsack.

"I'm sorry but to me, laughing like that in public, that's what I call skanky behavior."

They exploded in chorus.

"Oh no, we're not skanks."

"You don't say that, m'sieur."

"I didn't say you were skanks, I said that at that moment you were acting like skanks."

"All right, no way you call us names."

"'Iss not right, m'sieur calling us."

"The word isn't 'call', it's 'insult.'"

"'Iss not right insulting us that we're skanks."

"It's 'insult' by itself, or 'call us something.' But not a mixture of the two. Either I insulted you or else I called you skanks, but not both at once."

"Where you get off calling us skanks? That's not right m'sieur."

"That's enough, that's it, okay, fine, we stop right there."

Lina tumbled in, all smiles. To the sole colleague who happened to be there, she called a greeting that invited conversation. Her morning classes had gone well and she wanted to tell somebody. She came over to burrow for nothing special in her locker, wound up sitting down nearby. My scissors tripled their zeal.

"Ooh my oh my! Isn't he the busy one!"

If there'd been a response, she wouldn't have heard it.

"Interested in an orange?"

"Seville?"

"You betcha."

She pulled two out of her bag and took the smaller one, which she began peeling as she looked for the crack in my wall, a way to start up.

"The 9-Bs were supergood this morning."

"Yeah?"

"I even got a little bit of Spanish out of them."

"Anything can happen."

"The other day the dean came to the class for twenty minutes. We were trying to figure out what wasn't working. Suddenly today I changed my method a little. At the end I asked the kids if it was better that way. They said yes. So then I understood—not so much analysis of the texts. Now there won't have to be some inspector coming in."

She opened her locker, pulled out a few sheets of paper that she scanned in a second.

"Oh damn."

I stuck out my tongue as I smeared glue on the back of a grammar exercise. She tried again.

"This is stupid."

And again.

"This is really dumb."

"What's really dumb?"

She came over and sat down.

"I assigned them to write a biography of someone famous, and I look and see Calderòn. At first I had high hopes, but no, actually it's not Calderòn *Calderòn*, not *the* Calderòn, it turns out it's some I don't know what, some athlete apparently."

"Soccer player."

"So, I had a false hope, I guess."

She closed the locker.

"Really dumb."

Christian the dean of students was doing his best to collect the last stray 9-cs parked at the bottom of the stairwell waiting for the teargas to clear. As he maneuvered he called me over. He smiled, minimizing the issue in advance.

"We should meet at noon, if you can. There are some ninth grade girls complaining about you."

His saying it in a jovial tone irritated me.

"What girls? What about me?"

"Oh nothing, you know how it is, supposedly you called them skanks."

"Who said that? Sandra and Soumaya, is that who?"

"I don't remember really. There are a couple from 9-A too."

He was trying to tone down the drama, and I was boiling up in proportion.

"What do you mean, 9-A? It had nothing to do with anyone in 9-A, that business."

"I don't know, anyhow you know how it is, they say whatever they want."

"But what, you're refusing to tell me who it was, those ones from 9-A? I mean that's nuts!"

Given permission to move, the front of the flock broke into noisy action. Christian went back to take over as cowboy.

"You'll have to excuse me, François."

Moving around at the edge of the horde, Sandra was electrifying it. I nearly grabbed her by the down jacket.

"Come over here a minute."

My look must have been commanding because she complied without objection.

"I hear you went complaining about me to the dean, wonderful, thanks a lot."

She stammered guiltily.

"Well, yes, so?"

"You couldn't come tell me directly what was bothering you?"

"It's because you called us skanks."

"First of all I did not call you skanks, as you say, and second, the least you could do was come see me first to discuss the problem."

"If it's us, when the teachers wanna complain they go right to the dean, I don't see why we shouldn't go to him when you do something wrong."

"Well no, that's not a very logical deduction. It doesn't work the same in both directions, believe it or not."

I had markedly raised my voice. A group formed around us, among them Soumaya, who left it to Sandra to field my shots by herself.

"Naturally we're gonna do the same thing when we have a problem, otherwise it'd be too easy."

"And what did you expect to get from it?"

"What?"

"From going to see the dean, what did you all think would happen? That he'd punish me?"

"No. I dunno."

"What were you expecting?"

"Nothing, it was just to let him know, that's all."

"You were expecting him to punish me?"

"Acshully you shouldn't complain because at first we were going to tell our parents."

"But you should've done that, why didn't you do that? I'll expect them."

"Ohmigod don't say that, my father he finds out you insulted me a skank he'll kill you, I swear to you on the heads of my children from later on."

My mouth was gummy from a bad night's sleep, but it was coming at me hard as a machine gun.

"First off, you don't say 'insulted me a skank,' you say 'insulted me,' or 'called me a skank,' but 'insult me a something' is wrong, start by learning to speak French if you want to pick a fight with me. Secondly I didn't call you skanks, I said you were behaving like skanks, that's completely different, can you even grasp that or not?"

"Anyhow the whole school knows about it."

"Knows about what?"

"That you insulted us skanks."

I screamed in a low voice, teeth clenched.

"I did not call you skanks, I said that at a particular moment you were behaving like skanks, if you don't understand the difference, you're completely off your rocker you poor thing."

"You know what that is, a skank?"

"Yes I know what a skank is, so what? The question doesn't even come up because I didn't call you a skank."

"To me a skank I'm sorry but it's a prostitute."

"But that's not what skank means, not at all."

"So what is it then?"

My lofty pronouncement ran into a little jam.

"A skank is—it's a girl, not a bad person, who laughs stupidly at things, in an ignorant way. And the two of you there in the Administrative Council—at a certain moment you were acting skanky. When you burst out laughing that was like skanks."

"To me, that's not what it is. To me a skank is a prostitute."

She called to witness the circle of girls who had blissfully been watching me squirm for the last five minutes.

"Girls, does 'skank' mean prostitute or what?"

They all agreed. I turned on my heel and plunged into the stairway. My eyes suddenly stung.

Souleyman was wearing his hood pulled forward and the knit cap underneath it. Probably absent the previous period, Hossein greeted him by hammering Souleyman's right fist with his own left one.

"Souleyman, take all that off."

Dico took a while to unpack his things. He gazed at me as he considered something, then went ahead.

"M'sieur I got a question but if I ask you it you gonna send me to Guantanamo."

"Ah, am I?"

Only his neighbor Djibril, FOOTBALL POWER in a half-circle on his torso, was following the exchange, and he said,

"It's a real hot question, m'sieur. I swear on the Koran you're gonna send him right to the principal's office after."

"Did I ever do that before?"

FOOTBALL POWER.

"No, but m'sieur his question is way hot."

"So ask it already, get it over with."

"No, no m'sieur, you're gonna get real pissed off."

"We talk correct French here."

"You're gonna get real mad."

"Do I look like someone who gets mad?'"

"Sure do."

"You can't retreat now."

He fidgeted in his seat, grinning awkwardly.

"Some people, they're saying . . . no, drop it, it's over."

I had understood from the start.

"They're saying what?"

"Some people say you like men."

"They say I'm a homosexual?"

"Yeah—yeah that's it."

"Well I'm not."

"Them people that say it, they swear it on their life."

"Well, then there's gonna be some more dead folks."

"It's just some story?"

"Yep, sorry. If I were homosexual I would tell you, but I'm not."

Frida called out.

"M'sieur, how do you write 'qu'est ce que c'est'?"

Writing it out on the board, shaping the letters carefully, I felt it was an impossible expression.

"Why do you want to know that?"

"It was in the assignment."

Lydia had more acne than usual. Mohammed was laughing to himself over something or other. I would try to get out of this with the complement of the indirect object.

"Before we go on to correct the compositions, who remembers what a CIO is?"

No one.

"No one?"

Khoumba knew but wouldn't talk.

"Dico, give me a sentence using a CIO?"

"Me I dunno."

"Yes you do."

"I don't, that's all."

"Well, for instance, in 'I sold my car to a homosexual,' the phrase 'to a homosexual' is the complement of an indirect object—a CIO. It completes the verb 'sold.'"

"Pfffh."

FOOTBALL POWER.

"M'sieur that's messing with us too much."

Haughty indifference from me.

"And what do we do when we want to replace the complement with a pronoun? Anyone know?"

No.

"No one?"

No one.

"Well really."

Khoumba knew but she wouldn't talk.

"When we want to use a pronoun in place of a CIO, like for 'I dreamed about my recent travels,' we'd say 'I dreamed about *them*.' 'I often think about my job,' becomes 'I often think about *it*.'"

Hadia did not raise her hand before asking what was only half a question.

"Yeah but how do we know which?"

"I ask you the same question."

I needed a moment to think.

"*I* don't know."

Now I remembered.

"It's easy—complements that are introduced by '*à*' take '*y*,' and those introduced by '*de*' take '*en*.' There are exceptions, but when they occur, intuition will settle it."

She went on in the same tone.

"What's 'tuition'?"

"Intuition is when you do something naturally, spontaneously. For instance, some people use '*y*' or '*en*' without thinking it comes naturally to them. Fine, but for people who don't have intuition, there are rules as well."

A student pushed open the blue staff-room door without knocking. Bastien swallowed his cookie in a gulp and asked him to knock and to wait until someone authorized him to come in. The student closed the door and did as he was told, but no one followed up. Rachel was in her red shoes with the thick heels, and in good form. Reaching for the sugar canister, Sylvie asked about her absence the day before. The interested party smiled, pausing between her words.

"It was for religious reasons. It was Yom Kippur."

In vain, Sylvie shook the sugar canister over her tea mug. No more concerned than anyone else, Rachel ignored the knocking at the door.

"My children like it. And my husband's background is Arab, so they're doing Ramadan this year, too."

The smile never left her face, which showed faint discomfort as much as pleasure at talking about it. I asked if Yom Kippur was a Palestinian holiday consisting of surprise attacks on Israel every year. Rachel did not laugh.

"It's just a fast, is all."

Neither did Sylvie.

"Did you fast?"

"Yes."

"That can't be easy."

"No, but it's also a day of rest."

Marie took the great national debate down off the bulletin board.

"We've got to do something about the 7-AS, they're a catastrophe. I counted fifty-seven incident slips and thirty-four suspensions from all the teachers together."

"Team members should be getting together."

Gilles had a gray complexion and shadows under his eyes stretching to his earlobes.

"That won't change a thing. The eighth grade is the same, what can you do?"

"You look really tired."

"Yeah, I dunno."

Elise came in with a grin out to her ears, closing the door against the tireless knocker.

"They really are incredible."

Big grin.

"I'm walking through the courtyard, Idrissa comes up and he says, Oh ma'm, you're too pretty. I say, Well my lord, Idrissa, what's gotten into you? That's no way to talk to your teacher, I mean really. He says Yeah but ma'm you are looking too pretty with your new hairdo, all made-up and all."

Gilles was not grinning.

"Anyhow, I dunno, the sixth-graders, you get them the next year in seventh, and a year later in eighth, and a year after in ninth. It's still the same kids, they don't change."

Marie tossed the schools debate into the trash. The student's head reappeared in the doorway. Bastien was watching for him.

"What were you told? You were told to wait."

"No, you told me I must knock and then you will tell me if I can come in."

"And so? Did I say to come in?"

"But the science teacher, she the one say I got to come."

The science teacher was Chantal, who had a chocolate chip crumb stuck to her lower lip.

"That's so, I did ask him. I wanted you to get your home-note booklet signed, Baidi."

"My parents not here."

"How come?"

"They back home in the bled. In Algeria."

"And you have no brothers or sisters?"

"*Wesh*, I got my big brothers."

"First of all, we don't say '*wesh*,' and second, get your older brothers to sign."

"They not here."

"They're not here?"

"No, they in the bled."

"Okay, listen, you figure it out, what I want is for it to be signed by Monday."

She closed the door on Baidi then turned back, shaking her head."

"I swear. "

Jennyfer was whimpering about getting a five out of twenty and being comforted by Habiba, who had gotten a four. Hakim let his paper, marked seventeen, be passed along from desk to desk till it reached Lydia, her nails on one hand painted black, who had not taken off her down jacket.

"That guy, showin' off like he's the one did it when it's his big sister she does it all."

"You shut your mouth you."

He stopped to turn off the cellphone ringing at his neck.

"Do I confiscate that, Hakim?"

"No, no, don't bother."

I asked them to open their assignment pads to the next day, Tuesday, then began dictating the assignment. Aissatou and Faiza shot a glance at each other and wrote nothing.

"What's going on, girls?

"We're not in tomorrow."

"What do you mean, you're not in?"

"Tomorrow is Aid."

Soumaya looked up in the back row.

"I'm not sure it's tomorrow."

Ten kids began debating the question. I tried to control the tumult of divergent hypotheses.

"What are the chances it'll be tomorrow?"

"Ninety percent."

"Ninety-nine percent."

"Can't tell."

"Yes, it's tomorrow."

"Gotta check the moon, that's the thing."

After a couple of cacophonic minutes I cut it short.

"Who won't be here if it's tomorrow?"

Only five didn't raise their hands.

"Okay, turn your pads to Thursday."

Alongside my uniformed father, this detail, which was after all fairly commonplace, nonetheless conferred on the photo its singularity.

I gave them ten minutes to pick out the direct and indirect objects in the sentence. After ten seconds, Fayad raised his hand.

"What's that mean, 'conferred'?"

"'Conferred' is like 'gave'—it means 'gave the photo its singularity.'"

All the others crossed out what they had begun to write. Salimata raised her hand, three bangles on each arm, four necklaces around her neck.

"What's 'singularity' mean?"

"It means originality. You understand 'originality'?"

"Yes, that means something is beautiful."

"No, it means that a thing is particular, unusual. Here, it means that this detail gave an unusual quality to the photo."

When Alyssa ponders, her pencil suffers for it and the world grows lovelier.

"What did you say it means, when a person goes to see *un particulier?*"

"Oh my, that's a whole different thing. That's going to mix us up."

Mezut didn't need *un particulier* in order to get lost.

"M'sieur the sentence where does it start?"

"Please, really, Mezut. The sentence is the whole thing I've written on the board. It begins with the capital letter and it ends with the period. Please."

They set to work again, more satisfied than I was.

Sitting beneath the two painted peasants, Rachel felt that it was just not right.

"They can celebrate Aid, fine, but when they take advantage of it to skip two days, that's not right. We're left here with a class of six, does that make any sense?"

Nibbling at a cookie, Bastien was listening with one drowsy ear and, fact is, didn't give a hoot. Moving toward the lounge corner, Christian the dean distributed to whoever was there a typewritten sheet.

> My very dear colleagues, I take the liberty of soliciting you to come to the aid of Salimata, a student in 8-A who has just lost her father. He was vacationing at home in the Comoro Islands and was about to return

to France. He was buried there in his homeland, so it was impossible for Salimata and her family to attend the funeral. The price of a plane ticket is on the order of 1200 Euros, so it is most likely that Salimata will not be able to go there very soon to join her kinfolks. Such a visit is an essential condition for beginning the work of mourning. This is why I am asking you to kindly contribute some financial help to the student and her family by depositing money in an envelope reserved for this purpose in the administration office. Salimata is a most serious student and deserves our sympathy and compassion."

Rachel had not yet come to the end of her rant.
"Aid is one day long, period. People shouldn't abuse it."
Elise was willing to pick up the lost ball on the bounce.
"Say what you want, but for me, having only six students in 7-A would suit me fine."
The ball was in Julien's court.
"I think it's disgusting, I didn't have them yesterday or today. Was that the bell?"
He knew it was, if only from looking at Bastien, who had stood up, flinging off the cookie crumbs that clung to his sweater.

I had already scolded her twice. She still wasn't doing it.

"Ndeye, get to work."

"I wasn't talking."

"And you're also not copying down the definition on the blackboard."

"It's done, I copied the whole thing it's fine."

"You want me to come look?"

"If you wanna."

That last retort in a defiant tone. I took a couple of steps toward the rear of the room.

"You really want me to come look?"

"Sure, fine."

Same tone, INDIANAPOLIS 53 mounded up by her bosom. I moved forward a little more, just enough to see the lines written on her notebook page. I turned away.

"What I want is for you to be quiet."

"But I wasn't talking!"

"I said be quiet."

I erased the board to contain myself.

"Pffh."

"And I don't want any mouth noises either."

She did it again.

"That's it, you go out in the hall now and see me after class. I'll have a surprise for you."

She stopped her Pffh. Alyssa had something else on her mind, her eyes shaped in a question mark.

"M'sieur, when you sposed to use the semicolon?"

"That's rather complicated. It's more than a comma and less than a colon at the same time. It's rather complicated."

"Well all right but what's it for?"

"It's not worth complicating your life too much with that."

"Why did you put one on the board?"

The conditional MOOD is used to express something HYPOTHETICAL; the conditional TENSE is a FUTURE IN THE PAST.

"Yes, but well, it's complicated."

Fayad was not thinking about either the semicolon or the conditional, nor about the hail outside, nor the period bell that set the feathers flapping and brought Ndeye back. She passed his desk, HAPPINESS IN MASSACHUSETTS, and came up to hand in her home-note booklet where I had written Write your apology in 20 lines.

"Why would I apologize?"

"Because you pick these two-franc fights over nothing."

"I do not pick fights, why do you say that?"

"I know what I'm saying."

"Besides it's not francs now, it's euros."

"What do you care? You'll never have any money."

Hadia had been listening as she shrugged into her knapsack.

"You're always riding us, m'sieur."

"Somebody asked you anything?"

"No."

"Good."

"But lots of people think you ride us too much."

"And you, what do you think?"

"Me personally?"

"You personally."

"I do think you ride people too much."

"Yes, but you don't like me."

"Well, yeah, that's true I don't like you much."

"Well I don't like you much either."

"Sorry but the eighth graders are really the pits."

Gilles' remark reached only one of Bastien's ears, as he looked for a place to plug in the copy machine.

"The 7-AS are worse. We've got to have a meeting of the whole team."

"On top of that they're twice as crazy during this time of year, the eighths."

Bastien gave up on photocopying.

"Very sorry but the 7-AS—it was about time Ramadan ended."

On the cork bulletin board, someone had tacked up the photocopy of a document titled Reform of School Grading Notices—a parody. The lefthand column listed the subjects, the middle column showed student evaluations "Before Reform," and the last column "After Reform."

	BEFORE REFORM	AFTER REFORM
FRENCH	Spelling level a disaster	Jean shows great creativity and highly personalized handwriting
MATH	Written work: lacks rigor; oral work: nonexistent	Highly developed artistic sense; well-behaved student who keeps his own counsel
BIOLOGY	Unstable, scattered student; Jean is incapable of concentrating	The teacher apologizes for his inability to capture Jean's attention
ART	Far too often forgets to bring materials	Jean refuses to be a victim of the society of consumption

Lina returned from the washroom holding a cup by the handle. She collapsed into one of the armchairs, and this time she chose Geraldine, whose fifty-cent coin was being spurned by the coffee machine.

"Those 9-AS—they've done me in again."

"What a surprise."

"No kidding."

"It's Djibril, he says, Oh Spanish people they're racists. I tell him Listen Djibril there are racists everywhere, but there are no more in Spain than anyplace else. Then they all start hollering yeah it's true the Spanish people they're racists. Complete savages, I swear."

Geraldine fell back on a twenty-cent coin, which the machine would not swallow either. Lina blew on her tea, wrapped the mug in her two hands.

"I tell them listen, you can understand that it hurts me when you say that, because Spain is a country I love. Like a jerk I couldn't help reacting, you know?"

Not a ten-cent coin either.

"No kidding."

"Actually these kids are just as racist as anyone else. They have this anti-white racism—it's crazy."

"You wouldn't have any five-cent coins?"

"Yes, yes."

She straightened up to forage with a finger in a pocket of her jeans.

"Colonialism, okay, but enough already, there's a statute of limitations."

Geraldine was trying to cajole the machine with tender strokes.

"Like, I've got this Jewish friend, you know, well when it comes to the Germans she's okay about them now, she's not hung up anymore."

"Right, exactly."

Geraldine gave her back her fruitless coins.

Monsieur

I apologize for acting that way I get excited way too fast, and I am try to control that. I learnd that it was bad to act like I just did and so I will not do it anny more. Please acept my sinsere apologis.
Ndeye

Before leaving the room, Sandra unloaded a few volts on my desk.

"M'sieur is the republic a narrative?"

"You mean *The Republic*, the book?"

"Yeah."

"How come you know about it?"

"I'm reading it."

"Really?"

"Well yeah, I am, why?"

"Who suggested it to you?"

"My older sister."

"She's doing philosophy, your sister?"

"She's a biologist."

"That's very good."

"So is that a narrative, *The Republic*?"

"Actually, no, that would be more an argumentation."

"Oh?"

"You know Socrates, the guy who talks all the time in it?"

"Yes, yes, yes, it's always him talking, it's really funny."

"Well, he's an invented character—that is, no one knows exactly, so about him we can say he's like a character in a story."

"Did he exist a little?"

"Well yes, but no, anyhow that's not the most important thing. The point is mainly that he talks about all kinds of things with the people he runs into."

"Yeah, yeah, he never stops, it's really great."

"So Socrates is this guy who comes into the agora—the agora is a kind of public square where they all gather together—and there he listens to people and then he says to them, So—what was that you were just saying? Are you sure it's true, what you just said? That kind of thing."

"Yeah yeah, that's what he does I adore it."

"And so all right—they have discussions, it's like argumentation."

"Right."

"But really, it's terrific you're reading that, you know? Do you understand what you're reading?"

"Yes it's finc, thanks m'sieur goodbye."

"It's weird because usually that's not a book for skanks."

She looked back and smiled.

"Well yes it is—goes to show."

Unsnapping his metal pencil case to pull out ballpoints he would not be using, Dico whispered some parody of Chinese in the direction of Jiajia, who was already in her seat. Sharp sounds with a good many *l*'s. She did a poor job of pretending not to hear him, suppressing a look of anguish and powerlessness. If she'd been able to speak, she would have counterattacked. While the class settled into place, I bent over him.

"I thought people like you would know better than to do that racist stuff."

"I'm no racist, no way you can't say that."

I moved closer. Our eyes touched.

"I didn't say you're a racist, try to understand before you yell, I said people like you would know better than to do racist things."

He yammered another objection while I went back to my position, asking the students to take out a sheet of paper and their corrected compositions.

I made a column for vernacular terms that can be spoken but shouldn't be written, and beside it a column with their acceptable alternatives. On the left: bawl out; on the right: scold, reprimand, or berate. On the left: the pits; on the right: poverty, hardship, or joblessness. On the left: MacDo; on the right: MacDonald's, or fast food. On the left, supergorgeous; on the right: very lovely, or dazzling, or magnificent, or superb.

"Also avoid writing '*too* beautiful.' If you want to say very beautiful, say very beautiful. But not 'too beautiful. 'Too' doesn't mean 'very'; it means 'too much.' It's pejorative, you see? When I say I've eaten 'too' much, it means I've eaten more than a reasonable amount, that I might even get sick from it. And if I say I've eaten 'too well,' it doesn't mean I'm satisfied, it means that—I don't know—that it's shameful to eat so well when there are people in the world who never have enough to fill their bellies. See?"

"What's that mean, pejative?"

Frida spoke without raising her hand. I should not have answered since in doing so I too was breaching the community's rules of order.

"Pejorative means negative. A pejorative judgment is when you criticize someone. For instance, if I say that Dico's an idiot for not going over the corrections on the essay, that's pejorative."

In fact, he hadn't even pulled out his paper, settling for sounding a few intermittent Pfffh's.

When the period was over, he was the last to gather his things, perhaps intentionally.

"M'sieur, why'd you say I'm racist, I'm no racist, no way."

"So what is it then when you mock the Chinese accent? What is that if it's not racism?"

"I'm no racist."

"So what is that then?"

"Just to be funny."

"Really, it's funny? Do you think Jiajia is amused?"

"Sure she is."

He left abruptly as if ejected from his chair, denying me the pleasure of an implacable and poignant sermon I would have delivered.

Kantara was next up for consideration. Opinions had begun to course around the U.

"A whole trimester wasted."

"He doesn't do a thing—really nothing at all."

"It's the behavior, mainly."

"He is insufferable."

"Gab gab gab without a break."

The principal's gaze slid along the U as the comments progressed.

"So what do we do? Issue a warning?"

A collegial approval ran through the U. The principal prepared his pen.

"Warning about work or about conduct?"

The U split apart again.

"The work, at the minimum."

"Yes, the work."

"Well, and conduct too."

"Yes, conduct, it's the least of it."

"So, work and conduct, actually."

The principal pen was poised above the form.

"Warning on work and on conduct?"

A collegial approval ran through the U, the pen hit the form.

"Warnings on work and on conduct, noted. On to Salimata next."

"In sports she's an absolute gazelle."

"In math, more like a magpie."

The principal turned to those who hadn't yet delivered their diagnosis.

"So which is it? Magpie or gazelle?"

Leopold's sweatshirt showed only a unicorn whose nostrils flared with demonic venom.

"For me it's mainly the aggressiveness. It must come from her mother. I've met with her, she's the same way."

A gust smacked at the windowpane on the courtyard without troubling Geraldine.

"I think her father died in the middle of the term."

As dean, Serge knew more about that.

"As dean, I might be able to say more about that. Her father did die a month ago, but he had left their family home three years earlier."

Skeptical expressions from Jacqueline, Leopold, and Lina.

"Yes, all right, but that doesn't make much difference."

"I don't see her as traumatized, far from it."

"Anyway, her scores have been poor since back in September."

A parent delegate spoke up for the first time.

"I believe her scores have actually been dropping over the past three years."

Skeptical expressions from Lina, Jacqueline and Leopold.

"Yes, all right."

"As if by chance."

"That's a little facile, too."

Marking the form, the principal pondered.

Claude and Chantal were trying to talk down two boys tangling on the concrete of the interior courtyard. In my customary daze after four hours of classes, I didn't stop to think. Leaning over to separate them I pulled one by the hood and shoved off the other, who was still hanging onto the first. He fell backward onto his rear end and his head hit the ground. I thought Shit.

"No you don't no fighting like that!"

"Whatchu pushin me for?"

"What? What am I hearing? You using *Tu* to me?"

"Where you come off pushin me?"

The other pugilist had taken off, getting away from Claude and Chantal, who were watching me.

"You don't *tutoie* teachers!"

"Jus don't push me."

"You don't *tutoie* teachers, I said."

He tried to leave, I held him by the sleeve, snorting steam from my nostrils.

"Apologize!"

He arched his back and twisted free, I followed behind by three yards, and grabbed him again. Five or six times like that.

"Apologize!"

"Just don't push me."

"You don't *tutoie* your teachers."

I was talking between locked incisors.

"Apologize!"

A dozen students stood around us, along with Claude and Geraldine, who were open-mouthed.

"You want us to go get somebody?"

"No no it's fine leave me be. Apologize, you!"

He had got away again, I caught him in a couple of strides then held him with my one hand free of my satchel.

"Apologize."

"Why you always spittin on me?"

"I spit where I want to. Apologize."

"Why'dju push me?"

"Quit *tutoy*ing me."

I was yelling between clenched teeth, and the people scattered at the canteen door had gathered in a ring around us.

"What's your name?"

I was shaking him now, to get some word out of his mouth, anything at all to rescue me. The principal appeared over my shoulder.

"All right, Vagbema, what's going on here now?"

"He's been *tutoy*ing me for the last five minutes."

"What's that about, Vagbema, *tutoy*ing a teacher? What do you mean by that?"

"I'll let him go if he apologizes."

"Make your apologies, Vagbema. Apologize instantly."

"I apologize."

Without a word I let go, then slipped through the lobby door ten yards away. Behind me the principal went on with his sermon to save my ass.

"You're apologizing to whom? He has a name, that teacher, you know."

"I don know who that is."

They were either bored or sweating over a composition. Advance scouts for a storm, small horizontal spurts began to stain the windows. A first, a second, ten, thirty. I had never noticed that there were only three trees in the courtyard, if anyone had asked me I would have said four or five, visual memory is really something, like when you picture a Greek temple in your imagination, well you can't count the columns, if you were right in front of it you could but in the imagination it's impossible, drives you nuts, like a cat looking at its reflection or chasing after its tail, what's an animal's tail for? It must be for something, because everything in nature is there for some reason, although with a zebra's stripes it's not real certain, they say they're for attracting the opposite sex, but why not spots? And why spots rather than stripes on the coats of—

"M'sieur how you write '*égalité*'?"

That must be Khoumba asking, but she was hidden behind Dianka. I wrote the word on the board in capital letters to make it clearer. Djibril, FOOTBALL POWER, stood up before the others did. Deaf to my advice to look back over his work before turning it in, he laid his paper on the front desk.

SUBJECT

Following the model of the text studied in class, debate with a fictional character on the theme "We are not of the same world."

One day I'm taking the metro to get to school and I'm coming up from the train and I bump into some boy, it was a French boy it was his fault so I ask him to say pardon me. He answer me "we do not have the same worth." I answer him back "what way you so different from me" He answer me "I will tell you, while you are in your house sleeping me I am goin partyin while you goin to school me I am playin a video games that is the differens."

For that teacher in the courtyard.

Monsieur I am very sorry that I did not listen to you when I was fighting with my brother Désiré, and that I spoke to you calling you *tu*. That will not happen again. I beg you to accept my apologies. I behaved very badly toward you. Vagbema, 7-A

The half sheet of graph paper smelled of orange. I thought they must be making orange-scented paper these days, but when I took a textbook out of the locker it smelled the same. I reached my arm to the rear and felt about to find the fruit. Soon there it was, on my fingertips, soft and moldy.

When it precedes a *T*, the *I* in verbs ending in *-aitre* and *-oitre* takes a circumflex accent in the present indicative.

I finished writing and slapped the chalk dust from my trousers with hands covered in chalk dust.

"When you're done copying this, Abderhamman, you can come up to the board and conjugate the verb *croître*."

He stood up, wedged his waistpack squarely in the center beneath his NEW YORK JETS windbreaker, stepped over the foot Fayad had stretched into the aisle to trip him, passed by Alyssa whose face was a question, took up one of the chalk sticks lying on the metal sill. Hesitated over the first person. Over the second. Over the third. Wound up writing something that he then erased.

"I dunno m'sieur."

"Sure you know. Start by checking your endings."

Alyssa frowned, and he replaced the *t* with an *s* at the end of *je crois*.

"There, you see, now it's fine, and you remembered the circumflex accent for the third person. Go on."

He wrote *nous croîtons vous croîtez ils croîtent*. Alyssa frowned.

"You can go to your seat now, thank you. At least we can say he's consistent, because wherever there's an *i* before a *t*, he puts a circumflex accent. So that's good. Abderhamman, you paid attention to the rule. The only problem is that we don't say *nous croîtons*. What do we say?"

I'd addressed the question to the whole group, the whole group remained silent.

"What is the noun that comes from *croître*? It's a term in economics."

With their mouths they all shaped *crrrr* . . . sounds, looking for a vowel to end with.

"It's mentioned a lot these days."

"Christmas?"

"No, an economics term."

"Money?"

"We're looking for a word that comes from the word *croître*."

"Business?"

"From *'croître,'* I said."

"Currency?"

"No. Mezut."

The *crrr* sounds had ceased, the energies lost heart. Alyssa raised her hand without ceasing to chew on her ballpoint, and the question hanging on her forehead flew forward to me.

"M'sieur, what does *'croître'* mean?"

"It's like 'grow.'"

"Why doesn't anybody ever say it?"

"Depends on who."

"Do you say it?"

"All the time."

Between me and any parent visitors who might turn up, I had added the width of a table to that of my own desk. That being the case, I'd had to unstick my bottom a little to point to each of the grades on Amar's report card for his father and mother. As the two did not match my gestures with their own, I thought for a moment that they couldn't read, though I had some recollection that they could. Given my doubt, I chose to carry on without the paper prop.

"Amar's a nice boy, there's no doubt about that, but with his constant chattering it's hard to know any more what to do with him."

Their sorrowful faces agreed. She was veiled, he not.

"As his head teacher, I believe he'll get over it naturally, we can't do anything about it, it will improve by itself."

They moved their heads both yes and no. I filled the silence.

"So you shouldn't get too panicky, I tend to think the problem will go away by itself. Don't hold it against him too much. He's nice. It will pass. All by itself."

They stood up as one. After shaking my hand, she furtively brought her own to her heart.

"Good vacation to you, thank you for receiving us. Be well."

Without waiting for my invitation, a white mother had settled into one of the two chairs.

"I want to talk about Diego."

"Well, I think we've got big problems with his chattering."

"Actually there's trouble with his father, are you aware of that?"

"No but the teaching team is unanimous about his chattering."

"The thing is, his father is trying to get back some of our property, he even sent over a bailiff the other day, you see the kind of thing . . . so of course all that disturbs Diego."

"He may be disturbed, but mainly he's very disturbing himself."

"Actually last year there was his grandpa's death, that upset him a lot and ever since he's had trouble concentrating."

"Yes, we've seen that. And I think that—"

"Actually that makes two male role models less for him all of a sudden, and naturally he tends to overinvest in you because in spite of everything you're an adult role model."

"Ah?"

"Actually in this kind of situation there's got to be a pact of filial attachment and modeling and since you haven't formed that with him, naturally he develops self-defeating behavior."

"What he's mainly developing is behavior that irritates everyone."

"He is in need. He lacks a bonding attachment and he's trying to create one."

"Yes I see."

I got up, signalling to the next person to come up. The white mother was slow to understand she was being dismissed.

"These are children first, then students, you should know that."

"Yes yes, goodbye madame. Hello, m'sieur. Please take a seat. You're Mister . . . ?"

Through the layer of accent, I recognized Fangjie's family name.

"Ah yes, Fangjie. All right now, with Fangjie, her French is not there yet."

Nor was the father's; he gazed at me, smiling and uncomprehending. Hand and facial gestures came to the aid of my words.

"French, not very good. Progress, fast. So, hard."

He smiled, took the report card I held out without glancing at it, smiled again.

"Goodbye m'sieur, thank you for coming in."

Smiled again as he passed Teddy's mother, who spontaneously introduced herself as such.

"All right I know Teddy doesn't act like he should, but you know it's very hard because his big sister died, and so it's very hard, she took good care of him and all and now she doesn't anymore, so that's the problem, she used to do all that math with him, when she had the time I mean because she worked at the market, because her husband worked down there and when he left, well, she didn't work anymore until when she found a job cleaning in a hotel, because me I can't work anymore with my heart so she had to, she had to take anything she could find, even if it was far away, at the beginning she would go there by bus but that made her come home too late, so she asked her cousin for a scooter, that's how she had the accident, Teddy told me he wanted to buy her a pearl necklace, I told him it's too late now my poor little boy."

A flat box of chocolates sat in the middle of the oval table, half its pockets empty, half still full. The hesitant fingers of Claude,

Danièle, Bastien and Leopold hovered wiggling above it, then landed on their chosen sweets.

"Dogs, not for me, no thanks."

"A cat, now there's a fine animal."

Leopold agreed.

"I used to have one."

"I still do."

"You're lucky."

"In the morning I adore it when he comes to wake me up purring."

"Mine was like that."

"But still it's awful when you've got to leave and he's purring around your legs, you feel even less like going to work."

Leopold agreed. Gilles didn't.

"Cats are hypocrites, they purr and the minute you've fed them you don't see them again for three days."

"You don't look well . . . ?"

"It's Christmas, that depresses me."

Leopold and Lina agreed.

"Yeah, tell me about it."

Marie had her head deep in the belly of the photocopier.

"It would be nice if Santa Claus would bring us the front-and-back page thing. Anyone know how that works?"

Claude was the first to react to the bell.

"So, Happy Holidays if I don't see you."

Danièle got up heavily.

"Okay, only three more hours."

Bastien fell into step with her.

"Only two for me."

Leopold fell into step with him.

"I got only one."

The room was nearly empty. Hasty footsteps sounded ahead of Danièle, who darted over to the box of colored chalk she had left behind.

"What, you still here?"

"Yep."

"You sleeping here over vacation?"

twenty-six

I stopped off at the brasserie. A toothless woman about sixty was dropping her ash at the foot of the copper counter. She asked the uniformed server the new price on Marlboros.

"Five euros."

"Damn."

"Gotta."

"We're smack in the asshole of winter."

Outside, Claude's back was walking along in the dark. I caught up to him in front of the Chinese butcher's, and put out my hand. He gave a thin but affable smile.

"Well?"

Together we pushed open the large solid wood door, then deposited a hello at the open office of Serge the student dean.

"Happy New Year."

In the interior court with its frozen trees, the custodian Mahmadou had leaned a ladder against the wall shared with the nursery school. He climbed six rungs, stretched his neck to improve the angle of view, seemed tempted to move to the other side, decided against it.

Behind the blue door, the staff room was empty except for Valerie checking her e-mail.

"Happy New Year and all that."

My locker no longer gave off its scent of orange.

"Good health above all."

Dico hung back from starting up the stairs after the others.

"M'sieur can we still change classes?"

"No."

"Could I get a different French teacher?"

"Get moving."

Most of the troop was waiting in front of the physics room. Frida was telling a tale that a semi-circle of girls was drinking in.

"I tell him the day you hit me I swear you will die, he was totally in a panic, he goes why you think I'm gonna hit you? I go my cousin she's—"

"OK, inside."

They all went in, spread through the rows, sat, quieted down. The room smelled of cleaning and of the damp of disuse. I asked Kevin to go get chalk from the teachers' room. He sighed by reflex but was glad to escape five minutes of boredom.

"It'll give you a little exercise."

He smiled as he closed the door behind him. On the left in the first row, Dico hooted.

"You don't even do any sports yourself, right?"

I pretended not to hear him, he raised his voice.

"I'm sure you're no good at sports."

Shouldn't pick up on it.

"I'm sure you're really bad at sports."

"You think so?"

"You're bad at sports I'm sure."

"You're sure?"

As I spoke I wiped my two hands over my face, to look casual. After which my glance fell on Frida's smiling gaze.

"Are you annoyed, m'sieur?"

"Why—do I look it?"

"You're all red."

"That's because I was rubbing my eyes."

"The sooner we start the sooner we get to eat our Christmas galette."

The principal waited till each of us had taken our place around the U. After a few general announcements, he set his ballpoint pen turning between his fingers.

"For my part, I'm not in favor of ninth-graders repeating the year. Remember that the *lycée* has the capacity to take in everyone, vocational and academic tracks combined."

I pulled out a sheet of paper. Gilles had been sick from bad oysters the week before.

"I'm sorry but I see some pupils in ninth grade who haven't even reached seventh-grade level, what are they going to do in *lycée*?"

The principal's pen rolled between his hands.

"You know, some students who are completely lost in middle school reveal some aptitudes when they get into vocational."

Bastien took up the torch.

"I'm sorry but why aren't students like that taken out of middle school earlier? The ones in 7-A, for example, they're not going to reveal anything at all."

The principal continued so as not to retort.

"I must also remind you that the Official Bulletin advises against giving the students lines of text to copy."

Some people took permission to speak for themselves, Leopold among them.

"I'm sorry but I remember that at the teacher training institute they said a very interesting thing, it stayed with me because for once there was something interesting. They said that assigning writing exercises as punishment would associate the exercise with punishment in the students' eyes and they could come to see all exercises as punishments. So, taking it from there, giving lines to copy is no worse."

Geraldine took over the baton.

"Besides which, we're in a school where the kids don't know how to write, so you assign them a writing exercise to do and they give you back a few dog droppings. At least copying fifty lines is fifty lines."

The monitor Pierre appeared, carrying the Christmas galettes in a basket hanging from his arm. The principal continued so as not to retort.

"You know that there's virtually the same problem about giving warnings and reprimands in the class council. They are simply not legal."

Lina, who thirty minutes later would be saying Oh I got the hidden bean in my galette! and would unresistingly let herself be crowned with the cardboard tiara, said

"If that's the case, the kids can go right ahead and pull any crap they want, they know in the end nothing will happen to them."

I noted down: any crap they want, in the end nothing.

The DS that he owns lost a wheel.

"All right now, where is the relative clause in this sentence?"

Born January 5, 1989, Abderhamman spoke up.

"M'sieur, what's a DS?"

!!!

"Everybody knows what a DS is, I mean really . . . who'll explain to Abderhamman?"

Bien-Aimé, cellphone hanging at his neck.

"The uh relative—it's 'that he owns lost a wheel.'"

"Yes, well not exactly, not all that. But what's a DS—nobody knows?"

Nobody.

"You see them in the movies sometimes. No?"

No.

"In *noir* movies, for instance."

Fayad, GHETTO FABULOUS BAND in capital letters on his sweatshirt.

"What're *noir* movies?

"It's those detective movies where things happen that're not always awfully nice, that's why they're called '*noir*.'"

"Why do they say '*noir*' and not, I dunno, 'blue'?"

"So people won't get them mixed up with a Smurf. So okay then—nobody cares about my DS?"

When Alyssa speaks, a sky opens on another sky opening onto another sky opening onto another sky.

"M'sieur why did you say that what Bien-Aimé said isn't right?"

"I didn't say anything, he didn't give an answer."

"Yes he did, about the relative thing."

"Oh yes—it's because the relative clause ends after 'owns,' after that it's the rest of the principal clause, separated from the beginning: so you have 'The DS lost a wheel.'"

Hadia, black cloth wrapped and knotted at her neck.

"You didn't tell what that DS thing is."

"You can look it up at home. We're going on to the next sentence."

For the second time this year, Ming raised his hand.

"She goes to the movies with her friend that he is free."

I hoped that it was just a pronunciation problem.

"Come up and write your sentence on the board, that way we can see better how it works."

He stood up, courageous and concentrated, red sweatshirt with a white puma leaping across it. He wrote, "She goes to the movies with her friend that he is free." I sent him back to his seat.

"Thank you. Now then, the number of verbs is perfect, there are two of them so we do have two separate clauses. And also, we do have both a main and a subordinate clause, as I wanted, so that's very good too. The only small problem is you've put 'that he is' rather than 'who is.' It's correct to have a relative clause—it completes a noun—and not a conjunctive, which would have completed a verb."

Frida had certainly seen that I was waiting for people to get in line, yet she was hanging ten yards back with another girl. After ordering the others to start up the stairs, I strode the few steps that separated me from her.

"Frida, doesn't it bother you to make me wait this way?"

She didn't answer, but gave her pal a quick kiss and a "see you later," then started a stroll toward the staircase which my remark stopped short.

"Hey! I don't much like people blowing me off."

"Whad you say?"

"When I tell you to get upstairs, you get upstairs pronto, and I don't wait around while you give your girlfriend a kiss."

She stared at me with a look of defiance drenched in great contemptuous indifference. I'd slept badly, and I'd said "pronto."

"For me, a couple of little chicks strutting their stuff—I absolutely do not go for that."

She was startled but didn't blink, and went on her way with a faint shrug.

An hour later, when the bell emptied the chickencoop, I asked her to stay after for a couple of minutes. She thought What's he want now that jerk?

"Okay, just now downstairs I scolded you some and I was right to do it because it's exasperating dealing with these little two-bit challenges, people saying Not me I don't shape up just because the teacher says to. So I was right to be angry with you for that, but I did use some expressions, one in particular, that I'm not very happy with, and even not very proud of to tell the truth. So now I'm apologizing. I apologize for using those words, it was stupid and it doesn't mean a thing, I apologize for it. But from now on I really would like you to shape up at the same time as everyone else, okay?"

In the midst of my tirade she smiled her lovely smile of elegant kindness, and since I'd slept badly, my words twisted me up with emotion, and she said Okay.

Seated alongside me, Rachel's voice took on a confessional tone.

"I wanted to talk to you about something."

"Oh?"

"Monday there was a clash with the 9-cs. I heard Hakim call Gibran a dirty Jew because he wouldn't give Hakim a sheet of paper, so I called him on it, I said that it wasn't right, and the whole bunch of them went into a tailspin, it was chaos for a half hour, I'm telling you, I couldn't get them to understand what I meant, it was hell. When they left, I actually broke down, you know? I can't keep my cool on that subject. Since I'm right on the front lines, I just can't handle it."

"Ah?"

"Maybe you could."

"Who knows."

"Sandra is the one who really disappointed me. She said 'Well, me, I'm racist about Jews and I will be all my life.' Do you have them today?"

"No. Not till the day after tomorrow."

"Will you try?"

"We'll see."

Danièle had not budged from the telephone booth for a half hour.

"Yes, hello, I wanted to talk to you about your son, and invite you to a meeting we're having next week."

Geraldine, with her little lickable breasts, had just walked in.

"What are you doing?"

Danièle covered the mouthpiece with her hand.

"I'm calling the parents of the students in 7-A. I won't tell you the whole mess."

Gilles could have made himself a necklace out of the shadows under his eyes.

"Nyhow it's too late, they're not gonna change now. Same with the eighth graders."

Leopold, EVIL'S WAITING FOR YOU on his sweatshirt.

"Listen, the 7-AS are much worse. Did the bell ring?"

He knew perfectly well it had, since Sylvie and Chantal were scooping the sugar from the bottoms of their mugs with their stirring sticks.

"I used to dance, but I quit."

"I did too, for five years, but now I play the accordion."

"That's great!"

"Yeah, really. The music from Eastern Europe—it's got some absolutely fantastic bits."

Chantal stopped talking, I started.

"To me the accordion—it sends me up the wall. It reminds me of when I was a kid. The minute I heard it I used to get the feeling I was depressed, and I wasn't the slightest bit depressed. Sometimes we'd go to Sunday street fairs, the accordion playing over and over would give me these bottomless blues. It's a machine for manufacturing sadness, that crap instrument."

"That depends. For instance the music from the East is super gorgeous."

"East or West, it's awful. Music for hanging yourself. It should be outlawed. That's all."

a) Find the conjugated verbs in the text.

b) For each verb, state the tense and function.

After five minutes, Mezut had written not a word.

"How about we get to work now, Mezut?"

He emphatically uncapped his ballpoint and pulled up his chair with the zeal of an employment interviewee.

"Yes, yes."

They labored on in silence. The naked trees in the courtyard were still hard as marble in the icy wind. *Do as I say not as I do because the shit's so deep you can't run away. I beg to differ on the contrary, agree with every word that you say. Talk is cheap and lies are expensive, my wallet's fat and so is my head. Hit and run, and then I'll hit you again, I'm a smart ass but I'm playing dumb. I have no belief, but*

"M'sieur, what I wanna say, is 'their' a verb?"

"I beg your pardon, Mezut?"

"Is 'their' a verb?"

"Oh lord, really Mezut, 'their' is not a verb, I mean, please."

"Yes but m'sieur how can you tell it's not a verb?"

"I mean please, it's obvious, isn't it? A verb tells about an action; is the word 'their' an action to you?"

"Uh no."

"I mean really. Please."

At the start of the period I waited to see if they were calm enough. They were. I got out from behind the desk but didn't step down from the platform.

"Your art teacher tells me there've been some problems."

Sandra sighed, like, I can't take any more of this.

"Oh no, it's okay now."

"No it isn't okay. It isn't okay to have that kind of garbage in your head. I'm not going to bawl you out, I'm not going to give you a morality lecture, I'm not just going to tell you that anti-Semitism is bad the way smoking or breaking a vase is bad. I'm doing my job as a French teacher: I am warning you against inaccuracy. If you tell me that the complement of a direct object agrees with the auxiliary verb '*avoir*,' I'll tell you that's inaccurate. Well, disliking Jews is neither good nor bad, it's plain inaccurate. When I was your age, I was a communist—you know what that means, communist? It means roughly that a person is in favor of poor people being a little less poor and rich people a little less rich. But my enemies at the time, because at that age you've always got to have some enemies, my enemies were the bosses, the people who actually run things. That really did take a little more guts, no? and above all it was a lot more accurate."

Imani muttered something that got Sandra's exultant approval and they slapped palms.

"What's going on?"

"No no, nothing."

"Well yes, something is. You're laughing hard, so something's going on."

"No no."

"Yes. Tell me."

Imani hesitated, then began, looking me up and down, her nose barely masking a small obvious smile.

"Well that's just it, m'sieur, the bosses are the Jews."

There it was.

"Okay, I know that's what you think, and it's complete garbage. Or no, it's not. Actually what you mean is that the Jews in France are richer than the Arabs, and you know what? You're right. If you look at the average living standard of France's Jews, it is higher than the Arabs'. It's after that your garbage begins. It's when you deduce from that that they just took it all for themselves like thieves, and that they have the lust for money in their blood. That's what you think, isn't it?

"Sort of."

"Well that's complete garbage. I'm going to explain why in France the Jews are richer than the Arabs."

I gave three irrefutable reasons, ending with the culture of excellence, which you'd all do well to take for inspiration rather than be jealous of. Then I broadened the topic to what's going on in the Middle East, to make the discussion last rather than go back to the scheduled lesson. Three times fifteen-minutes-of-fame and the class bell didn't snap them out of their silence. The henhouse remained pensive, except for Hakim, who's an eight-year old politically, and Sandra, who came up to lean her naked little potbelly on my desk. A hundred thousand volts of energy divided by her contrition.

"M'sieur I'm really sorry I said that, I don't know what got into me, it was supposed to be humor."

"Just middling as humor."

Her knees jiggling in continous spasm, she waited for the departure of Jie, who was busy making Zheng recite the Latin subjunctive.

"Hey, we can see your underpants!"

And in fact a cotton band did show above his low-slung trousers.

"Was that humor too?"

"It's true though, we do see his underpants, no?"

"Is that all you want to say to me?"

Her big electricity-conducting earrings encircled half her cheeks.

"No, it was about next year. The other day I went to see the *lycée* Marcel-Aymé. M'sieur it's impossible, I can't go there, there's nothing but Goth kids there."

"Is that so?"

"Really. I swear it's true, there's just skateboarders, I could never talk to them."

"Well as long as they're not Jews."

She tapped her foot in exasperation.

"Ah c'mon, m'sieur, really, I said I was sorry. But I swear to you over there it's impossible, there's nothing but punks."

Leopold was trying to get the machine to take a fifty-centimes coin. Bastien finished eating a cookie and reading a sheet he found in his locker.

"You see this thing?"

In the lounge corner, Chantal was correcting papers on a thigh tilted up to make a desk.

"This one doesn't even write her name, she'll hear from me."

The remark was not addressed to anybody, but I was the only one sitting nearby.

"You know who it is?"

"Yes, but she doesn't put her name, that's going to be trouble."

Bastien could not get over it.

"Did you see this thing?"

Leopold banged the flat of his hand against the side of the machine. Chantal didn't notice.

"With me a paper with no name gets a zero."

I waited to be sure she wasn't joking.

"Zero, really?"

"You bet. How else can you manage?"

"You wouldn't have change for fifty centimes?"

"Did you see this thing?"

This time Bastien left me no choice, handing over the sheet.

REPORT FROM THE TEACHING AIDES

We were in the staff room, Clarissa, Amara, and Sylvaine, with the students from 7-A. Jallal El Moudena's big sister came into the room and asked her sister

"Who slapped you?" Jallal pointed to Ouardia Agadir, and the big sister started yelling at her and threatening her. Ouardia answered violently "Dirty ho, you just go back to getting screwed by everybody." The big sister then threw herself onto Ouardia and hit her. We were therefore obliged, Clarissa and Sylvaine, to pull them apart. Kinga went to get M. Giresse. With all the hitting going on, several times we asked the big sister to leave the room. But in vain. She continued to punch Ouardia, who fought back just as hard. We had to wait for M. Patrick to get the big sister to leave. We kept hold of Ouardia while M. Patrick took the big sister out of the room and out of the courtyard.

"Speaking of punk, did you know a group called The Black Tits?"

Leopold hadn't read the report and was taking up a brief exchange we had begun the week before.

"Yeah, yeah, I knew them."

"Well see, that's a group that made the transition from punk to Goth."

He opened Rachel's locker, where sometimes there were ten cent coins.

"And did you like that group?"

"Too much text."

He returned to the attack on the machine.

"Yes, it's true they were more into intimacy, personal, less political. It's less of a revolt against society than an individual revolt, I mean, it's more personal, more sentimental, more how shall I say . . ."

"Romantic?"

"Yeah that's it, as a revolt it's more romantic."

Walking ahead of me, Souleyman went into the room with his hood up.

"Souleyman."

He turned to me. Saw me point to my skull to symbolize his. Took off the hood.

"The cap too, please."

His scalp was now covered with an infinitesimal layer of yellow hair. I had them take out their assignment pads to note down a quiz for the following Thursday. Jie and the three other Chinese began exchanging grimaces of discomfort. After a whispered consultation, Jiajia was silently appointed spokesman. Her hand went up, and with a slow blink I invited her to speak.

"Thursday we are not be here, it is not possible for us do the quiz."

"And why won't you be here?"

"It is Chinese New Year because."

"And you can't move it?"

My smile did not spur her to see the joke.

"No no we cannot move. It not us who they decide."

"All right then, the other students please note that we'll do an hour of class discussion that day instead."

Over on the left, front row, Dico let out his hiss of disapproval.

"That's dumb, class discussion."

"What's that, Dico?"

"It's dumb, I'm not coming."

"What are you saying?"

"I'm not coming it's dumb."

"Say it again so I get it."

"I'm not coming."

"Repeat one more time so I get it."

"I'm not coming."

"You want us to go talk to the principal?"

"I'm not coming."

"OK, let's go."

I stepped down off the platform.

"Follow me."

I opened the door and pointed him to the stairwell with a thumb. He passed beneath my outstretched arm.

"The rest of you, keep it down."

I went down the hallway, he followed three yards behind.

"Hurry up."

He didn't. I stopped so he could move ahead of me. We went no farther. I gave in and passed him. In the stairway I went down three steps then climbed back up two to wait for him.

"Imbecile."

"Why you insultin me?"

"You're the one insulting the teachers, by answering back."

"Where you come insultin me?"

In the interior courtyard the distance between us grew still greater. We climbed the stairs that way up to the open office of Christian the dean. I didn't wait for him to finish talking to a student's mother with a translator beside her.

"I'm leaving you this maniac. I won't take him back next period without a written apology."

"All right."

"Sorry."

"No no."

Mechanically, the translator transmitted this last exchange in some African language, then clapped an embarrassed hand over her mouth.

Danièle came in blowing on her hands, though they were gloved, and took her seat with polite dispatch. Seven of twelve committee members present in the study hall rearranged for the occasion; a quorum thus reached, the principal could begin. By restating the facts:

"Ndeye was in the hallway at the end of the line. She was holding some small pink balls which I took to be candies. I asked her to put them away immediately. She refused. I asked again, she began to reply. At that moment, I requested her to accompany me downstairs to my office. She refused and called me, and I quote, a jackass. Once in my office, she calmed down, and later that afternoon she came back to apologize."

He paused.

"I note that, given the gravity of the facts, I was within my rights to lodge a formal complaint. I did not do so, for I consider that it is always best to first seek a punishment that is educational in nature. For that reason as well I believe that this Mediation Council can allow Ndeye to commit for the remainder of the year to conduct that is customary and respectful toward adults."

Her one-eyed mother whispered a few words to Ndeye in an African language. Her good eye was set on the speaker, whose uncomprehended remarks she had accompanied with approving murmurs.

"The temporary expulsion is therefore not the sole solution we propose. We will also ask Ndeye to spend two afternoons a week with the children at the nursery school next door, to put her in the position of an adult so that she may see the impossibility of doing anything at all without some agreement on common rules. Furthermore, we will ask that Ndeye be provided supervision by a psychologist."

The social worker broke the silence of the listening group.

"She's already getting that."

The principal suppressed a scowl of irritation.

"We will ask that such supervision be continued."

"**No, macho's not** the same thing, macho is a man who flexes his muscles and struts his maleness, and he treats women with a kind of contempt. But it's not the right word to describe men who don't like women, because actually, the macho guy does like women in a certain way. So how do we say that?"

"Homosexuals."

"Oh no, nothing to do with it, just because a guy isn't sexually attracted to women doesn't mean he dislikes them. On the contrary, homosexuals generally adore women."

Nonsense. Faiza, black scarf tied at her throat, "Of course—they're alike."

"Maybe. And what about my word, then—nobody knows it?"

I had written "mysogynist" on the board, then, on second thought, "misogynist."

"The prefix '*mis-*' is used as a negative, and '*gyn*' is connected to a Greek word that means '*uterus.*'"

I was confusing it with hysteria, but that wasn't the reason they broke up. Nor what caused Aissatou to speak.

"M'sieur people who want women to stay home all the time, is that misogynists?"

"Right, that's an example."

Yes, but, said Dounia, the woman also needs to be protected, Yes but, Soumaya said, keeping her home all day is abuse, Yes but look at porn movies, that's abuse too, said Sandra plugging into her electric grid. I say they should be forbidden because it's a lack of respect, and like I see it too, said Hinda who resembles somebody or other, sometimes you have these movies they're not even porn even there you got scenes with sex and all. Yeah I think so too, Sandra resumed, when I come across them and I'm with my father omigod I really feel so ashamed, so now when he says c'mon we're gonna watch television I say no, Yeah, said Soumaya or Imani or Aissatou, at least when you're back home in the bled you don't have to always be keeping your hand on the remote or whatever, in the bled you can watch and you don't worry but here it's not the same you always got your hand on the remote in case there's some sex or something, Yeah me in Egypt it's the same way when I watch television there I'm peaceful, I don't need to switch channels all the time but here in France it doesn't help they got so much weird stuff on all the time you know m'sieur?

"Yes."

Even before I mentioned my request, the principal insisted on telling me the latest.

"I've got to tell you the latest."

He was getting a kick out of the tale to come.

"You know that Ali, one of the monitors?"

"Yeah yeah, the one who's kind of heavy with square glasses."

"No, a thin guy with no glasses."

"Oh yeah, I remember."

"Well, by mutual agreement we have broken off our collaboration."

"Really?"

"He was here on trial, and let's just say the trial didn't work out."

He snorted with laughter again.

"Actually, for the month he's been here, it was never really functioning well. There were little clashes with the students all along, the current never really flowed between them, but still it was mostly anecdotal. Until yesterday."

He paused.

"Yesterday, he comes in here yelling 'I'm gonna kill them, I'm gonna kill them,' went on like that for three or four minutes. So we sat him down, I told him to calm down, that we'd talk it all over quietly. He finally stopped yelling. And then he starts laying out all his complaints against the students. I told him that in the circumstances it might be better if he looked for some other school, or even some other line of work, and he said that there was no doubt about it. Finally the whole thing was worked out nice as could be."

He looked for confirmation in my expression. Found it.

"Well, worked out—easy to say, because still I did have to take him home, and as we left the school I had to relieve Djibril of this object."

From between two cupboards he drew out a brass bar.

"All right, Djibril wouldn't have done much with the thing, and in fact he handed it over with no problem, but I mean you never know."

I was ready to bring up another subject, but he wasn't.

"On the way, I talked with Ali. I found out some wild things."

"Ah?"

"He told me that all through his childhood his mother had

always told him You you'll never amount to anything. Right there you understand a lot of things."

The smile was gone, and now, chewing on the earpiece of his glasses, he grew pensive, staring thoughtfully into my eyes.

Khoumba came in without knocking, one finger holding a cotton plug in her nostril, her chin slightly raised.

"Any better?"

As she took her seat without answering, Fortunée said something that made her smile. Suddenly Dico shouted to Mehdi from one end of the row to the other, I went Oh! He went What?

"Don't do that, okay?"

"What did I do?"

"You starting up again?"

"Why you talkina me?"

"You want to go back down?"

"I don't care, y' know?"

"Okay, we're going back down."

I opened the door and pointed to the staircase with a thumb. He passed beneath my outstretched arm. Once the door was closed, I changed my mind.

"On second thought, you're going to stay right here in the hallway. I don't want to waste my time over you."

"I don't care."

I pointed a finger under his nose and stared hard into his eyes.

"I don't need your comments."

"Why you mad?"

"Shut up."

"If I feel like it I'm goin back inside."

"Just try it."

He climbed back up the stairs behind me.

"What you gonna do to me if I go back in? You gonna hit me?"

"Fine, okay, we'll go to the office."

In the stairwell I walked down three steps and then back up two to wait for him. On the next floor we walked side by side, slowly or I'd lose him and that would be ridiculous. I searched for the most off-hand tone I could find among those available in my overheated brain.

"Isn't this nice, huh, walking along together?"

"Pfffh."

I mimicked a stroll in the countryside.

"Life is great, huh?"

"Pfffh."

The others were probably glued to the classroom windows watching us.

"Your life is nothing, Dico. Aren't you sick of your nothing life?"

I stopped for a moment to knock something off my shoe and thus legitimize our grotesque slowness.

"Pfffh."

One way or another we reached the office door.

"Don't be such a smartass in there."

"I don't care."

"Okay don't care but don't be such a smartass."

The principal wasn't in. Dico rejoiced silently.

"You sit down there, I'll go find him."

He didn't sit.

"You sit there and keep quiet."

"You're the one who's talking."

We were coming to the questions submitted by various members of the Administrative Council. The principal was managing things.

"The instructors would like to raise the issue of the coffee machine. On this matter, the best thing would be to ask monsieur Pierre to take the floor, and outline the financial issues."

Monsieur Pierre was already sitting perfectly erect in his seat.

"As to the machine, you recall that it was installed in the course of the 2001 fiscal year, because the preceding machine, which had to be restocked regularly and therefore required the services of a sub-contractor firm, was not profitable. That being said, the present machine has also turned out to lose money, which has led us to raise the price per cup by ten centimes, bringing the cost to fifty centimes."

The blue stripes of his white shirt remained impassive in the face of the discontented mutter provoked by his last line.

"In the circumstances there can be no expectation of a return to the earlier cost formula, which cannot balance the account."

The principal kept a sidelong eye on the rebellion about to burst forth. I burst forth.

"I believe there's some misunderstanding as to what we feel needs to change. It's not so much the machine itself as the fact that a shortage of coffee packets occurs more and more frequently. Two months ago, the problem came up only rarely, and we also had a far greater choice of hot drinks. For some time now, not only is there a diminishing quantity of coffee available, but furthermore there are no longer any packets of chocolate or containers of milk or tea. We are often forced to walk back to the storeroom ourselves for replenishments, making a number of trips that represent time lost from our strictly pedagogic activities. And moreover, the service people refer us to you, monsieur Pierre, because per your orders, they are no longer responsible for stocking the supplies. It would seem that there is some suspicion weighing on those personnel, particularly as to the sugar packets which, to judge by the figures, vanish into thin air. In short, it is no longer clear which saint we should pray to, and meanwhile it is not rare to find that there is no coffee in the morning, whereas within these walls it is a recognized fact that coffee is the nerve tissue of the war."

Little approving snickers—a bit of a turn-on—then a peace-making gesture from the principal.

"If you like, we'll come back to this matter, for we must go on to something far less world-shaking, more frivolous: the overall course schedule for next year."

He first spoke of his delight that it would be increased for this school, contrary to the situation elsewhere in the system. We then turned to the details. Following up some ideas discussed in the preparatory meeting, Marie suggested that the extra time should go to the language courses, and that for instance we might double the number of periods in eighth grade to allow for smaller groups better suited to oral practice.

The principal found the idea interesting, but objected that the plan would mean cutting a half hour of individual help, which would be tantamount to eliminating that program altogether since the students would then get only an hour every two weeks—so to speak, nothing at all. It was then proposed to add an hour of physical education at the same grade level, which, given the profile of this year's seventh-graders—who would be next year's eighth-graders—could go a long way to channel their energy, and start them off in a good dynamic, since after all it's just about the only course they can manage at all. But then were we abandoning the idea of consolidating English language training for eighth grade? No, the additional hours of seventh grade French could be joined together with the eighth grade French hours, since we know that the sixth-graders did very good work this year, and turned into language periods. That way our 407 hours, compared to the 400 of the past year, would be put to better use, though it would still be important to keep a small margin to cover for the uncertainties in the back-to-school arrangements.

An hour later, seven bottles of white wine stood erect on a table the monitor had scrupulously covered with a white paper cloth. I rushed back to the staff room to pick up a bundle of student papers, unsure whether I'd find the door still open. It was, but a flip of the switch did not turn on the light. The room was filled with shadows and then increasingly with total darkness as I moved forward, and it was only by the scent of orange that I was able to identify my own locker. I was feeling about inside it to locate the bundle of papers when the light came back on.

"Nothing gets done in a day."

It was that ageless voice from the custodians' closet. Stationed in the door frame, its owner gazed at me from the depths of his brain.

"But without a day nothing gets done."

He was missing an arm.

"You unhook the last car of a train, there is still another last car. You remove the first day, and the second is now the first. It always starts with one day."

I had begun to draw closer, but with each step I took he moved back by as much and soon he had disappeared.

Two sixth-graders with shaved heads were climbing the wall to retrieve a foam ball that a spirited shot had sent to the other side. Not a sound came from over there, as if there were nothing beyond, as if the world existed only here. The principal called me from his office where it opened onto the courtyard.

"Our friend Dico has written you some gibberish."

Taking the paper folded in quarters, I affected the easygoing cowboy.

"More Chateaubriand prose, I suppose?"

He laughed hard, then took an ironical tone.

"Every last word!"

The ball wasn't going to come back. It had taken off into infinite space. When I pushed open the blue door, Mohammed the monitor spun sharply about on his chair, as if caught in some act.

"Hello."

"Hello."

He turned back around and went on surfing on a mobile telephone site. I waited till I got upstairs to unfold the paper.

> Monsieur, I apologize for talking back to you in front of the 9-A class and especially for being so insolent to a teacher who has always been kind to me. I conclude by telling you that I promise to try to do better toward the teachers.
>
> Dico

"Would you have fifty centimes in tens?"

It was Lina, affable. I hadn't heard her coming over.

"Can't you remember to get change? Is it too much to ask you to think ahead a little about things? Improvising is nice, but when it doesn't work out it's other people who wind up paying. It's nuts to just float along mindlessly that way, shit."

I lowered my voice and took on the tone of a wild-eyed preacher.

"If they ever discover there's a gene for crime, that will change a lot of things. Because what will we do with people who carry it? For the moment, when people kill, we always say that it's partly their own doing but it's also caused by many other things—'mitigating circumstances,' it's called. We think that if we get them help, they won't do it again. But if they do have the gene in them, then it means they can't be cured, so what do we do then? Lock them all up, even before they commit a crime? Otherwise it's laxity."

Alyssa stiffened into an exclamation point, then twisted into a question mark.

"What's that mean, laxiddy?"

"Laxity, being lax, is letting things go by too easily. It's like indulgent, but negative. Like parents who let their ten-year-old kid hang out in the street at midnight. We also use the term 'permissive,' because they permit too much."

With the chalk I wrote *lax* = *permissive*. Alyssa copied it on the margin of her notebook.

"These days, for instance, there's discussion about whether school is a little permissive, if the school shouldn't discipline kids more, for example people like Mezut who keep turning around ten times an hour, huh Mezut?"

"It's because there's something I don't get."

"Oh?"

"Yeah, I don know what a gene is, m'sieur."

"Well I mean . . . I just explained . . ."

Bien-Aimé, WASHINGTON DC, knew the answer.

"It's when a person feels like killing and can't stop himself."

"Careful, though. Genes are not necessarily about crime. And I repeat that so far nobody has found a gene for crime."

Alyssa had begun darkening a sheet of paper, Mezut still didn't understand, Fayad was laughing over something, Hadia's plastic earrings trembled in time with her brain.

"Like what other kindsa genes is there, m'sieur?"

"Many. Maybe there's a gene for humor. Or for niceness. Or— I don't know—for spelling."

"M'sieur is there gonna be a—"

"—next Sunday, Tarek. Sunday morning we'll have a dictation. At eight a.m. Without fail."

The bell rang, the birds flew off, Alyssa handed me her sheet of paper.

"I wrote an argumentation."

"Oh?"

She slipped away before I read it.

Lax = permissive

Should we bring back the kind of authority our grandparents knew in school? I think that we should leave the past behind us and that things that worked well back then might be less effective nowadays and in the future. I think that an adult should state his position and lay down his rules according to his own values, not in the name of some system that would be come back into use and would consist of being more severe toward students. Although often in our schools there is a lack of diligence, of respect, and many other factors that is causing this reconsideration, would it be a good solution to restore the kind of authority that still lives on in the ways of the old-timers? I do not think so myself. Young people today would not accept such authority. They could not even imagine it. This new generation mostly does not like punishments, or constant heavy pressure, they feel they get enough of it. Moreover, there are certain countries, in particular those in the third world, that do apply this method of teaching in their schools, and I think I can say that students there would love to be in our shoes! So if the idea is to restore something out of nostalgia for the past, no!

Jihad detoured past my desk before going to his seat. Worried. Almost troubled.

"M'sieur, is Benin a country?"

"It certainly is, it's a country in Africa. In black Africa."

He threw a look at Bamoussa, who was listening at a distance, and I could tell some disagreement between the two was going to be arbitrated.

"But . . . what I mean, Benin, is that, like, a big country, m'sieur?"

Hanging on my lips, which were pursed in consideration.

"Well I'd say no, not a big country, but not small either."

I was pretty certain about not big, but as to small I had some doubt, which Jihad didn't pick up, pleased as he was to hear that there was nothing monumental about Benin.

"So it's not too big, then?"

"No, not too."

He turned to Bamoussa with the air of See I told you so. I turned him back toward me.

"I take it this is for a quiz in history class, is that it?"

"No, no, tomorrow Morocco is playing Benin, that's why I wanted to know if they're any good or not, the Benins."

"Medium, I'd say."

He flew to his seat.

Sensing that Jean-Philippe wanted to talk to me about the 9-AS, I pretended to be absorbed by my hyperactive scissors. Ignoring this, he leaned over my table.

"I had a little problem with your class."

"Oh?"

Chantal went by and grinned.

"So I hear there's a gene for crime? You've got them all worked up, they want me to give them a special class on it."

Nothing would divert Jean-Philippe from his tale.

"Last week, I got—well—some pretty weird messages on my answering machine."

"Oh?"

"Yeah, messages that were rather special, quote-unquote. Rather obscene, you could say. And well right away I recognized who it was. It was two girls, and I'm sure one of them was Dounia."

"All right."

He would have loved to go on. Geraldine was there with her pretty little useless breasts. Danièle entered the room exasperated.

"It simply cannot be allowed, we shouldn't stand for that. What's got into them today?"

Leopold didn't look up from his pile of student papers.

"What's going on?"

Danièle couldn't get over it.

"Don't you find them all worked up today?"

"No more than usual."

Bastien was distracted by a paper jam in the belly of the photo-copier.

"No more than any other end-of-the-week."

Danièle didn't let go.

"With the 8-as, the end of the week begins Monday afternoon. That parent conference was really worth the bother, sure."

"There should be another conference, with the whole team there."

"And a lot more Disciplinary Councils, especially."

Having spoken, Leopold and Bastien each dove back into, respectively, the composition papers and the copy machine. Beneath the painted peasants at prayer, Danièle was still furious.

"But no, really today there's something in the air, I'm telling you."

Julien turned away from the computer screen, where a bouquet of chalets gleamed in a valley.

"It may be the game."

That hit TILT for Bastien.

"Oh yeah sure! that's it, a little while ago I heard them talking about Mali-something."

I knew the something.

"Mali-Senegal, the quarter final of the Africa Nations Cup. It's being played in Tunisia this year. It's every two years. Cameroon holds the title."

Danièle was not letting it drop.

"Okay, fine, I don't exactly see what that has to do with the price of onions."

In the end, Bastien would not be making his xeroxes.

"They ought to declare school holidays on African soccer-match days, that way everyone would be happy."

Leopold finished writing down his red-marker comments. Fine work.

"Or else broadcast them in the classrooms and we could build the lesson around them."

Danièle would have none of it.

"Me and sports, I don't get it, especially team sports. My son tried to explain rugby to me but it's not worth the trouble."

And yet rugby is fascinating. Organizing chaos to produce power—fascinating.

As he sat on a bench in the early-dusk courtyard, Idrissa's red sweatshirt struck a sharp note. A crow croaking endlessly at the top of one of the three trees made me look up. On a bench beside the accused, Oussama's silhouette grew excited.

"Omigod, a crow—not a good sign for you."

A quarter of an hour later, Idrissa was sitting again, but now in the study hall rearranged for the purpose. The principal was reading the incident slip from the teacher of Life and Earth Sciences.

> "I asked Idrissa to take out his working materials, but he had nothing with him. He stood up to borrow paper from a girl nearby, and when she refused, he slapped her with his cap. I therefore asked the class delegate to go get the principal. Idrissa then said, 'That's right, go get God.' Then he stood up, came to the desk with a challenging look, and said, 'What are you (he said *tu*) going to do to me now?' He went toward the door, I asked him to stay

in the room, he said he 'didn't give a damn' and disappeared, slamming the door."

Looking up over his half-glasses, the principal greeted the culprit's mother, who, as he was reading, had parked a double stroller in an angle of the U and sat down. One by one he introduced each of the permanent members of the Disciplinary Council to her. At each name she gazed into their eyes and said "hello" as she brought her hand to her heart. The principal finished by asking that the boy be definitively expelled, and went on to say that if that was the decision, the penalty would have an educational value and would offer Idrissa the chance to build a new self in another setting.

As his head teacher, Valerie took the floor and explained that she had congratulated Idrissa for the great progress he had made recently, and that may have provoked him to a sense of overload that he tried to compensate for by the doing the opposite. A large gold cross hanging at her chest, the educator said that Idrissa had always been very polite with her, but that sometimes he was silent for a half-hour at a time. A parent delegate reminded the group that Idrissa had gone through the war in Angola and that would certainly affect the way he behaved. She insisted that the punishment be accompanied by a psychological evaluation. The principal said that, whatever the penalty to be determined tonight, it would be educational in nature. Marie suggested that a change of schools would do him the most good, that the situation here was terrible. While she was speaking, whether through cause and effect or not, Idrissa and his mother carried on a tense exchange in low tones. When Marie stopped speaking, we could hear the two of them without grasping the object of their dispute. She was arguing with him but he eventually stood up.

"Whatchu think, you think this here is paradise?"

He repeated this three times, left the room, and reappeared.

"You want to throw me out, throw me out. Fine and we don't talk about it no more."

The principal imperceptibly dropped his affable tone.

"Yes, in fact, Idrissa, we do have to talk about it. It's important to talk about it and important that you hear what we say."

Idrissa sat back down.

"I don't give a fuck."

The principal cut things short by offering the mother the last word, in conformity with the legal procedure. She said nothing; she was invited to await our deliberations in the adjoining lobby. She withdrew with thanks to us.

We voted for permanent expulsion.

Salimata put off looking at the paper dropped on her desk, then she stretched her neck forward and saw the four out of twenty grade.

"You absolutely have to be more careful with the way you put things, Salimata. That's the whole foundation, right there. Start by taking more care with your sentences, and after that we can talk about the rest."

Used to such grades, she gave no sign of disappointment.

"To start with, you have to take out all the expressions that are like talking, you understand?"

Her mouth shaped a soundless "yes." I picked up her paper again to illustrate what I meant.

"For example, with the negative of the verb, putting *pas* alone isn't enough, you have to put *ne*-something-*pas*." I exaggerated the stress on the '*ne*.' "And look—terms like 'super-cool'—it's not correct for writing, only for speaking."

She raised her empty gaze to me.

"Especially because oral—speaking—expressions are often exactly the ones where a person can make a mistake, because we're not used to seeing them written down, we only know them by ear, and the ear can fool us."

A salvo of my spittle landed on her pencil kit, scrawled in magic marker with MALI TO THE LIMIT.

"For example, we don't write 'zample' but 'For example.' And you don't start a sentence with 'or' or 'and' in writing the way I just did talking. You can *say* 'I did that before,' but you have to *write*, 'I've done that in the past.' There are things that are all right in speech but not in written French."

Alyssa, a docile pencil between pugnacious teeth, LOS ANGELES ADDICTION printed ten inches below, and skies opening in endless succession.

"But m'sieur how do you know if some expression is only okay for saying?"

I set down Salimata's paper to gain a little time.

"Usually these are things you just know. Things you sense—that's it."

Hadia sat up as if stung awake.

"It's tuition."

"That's right. Intuition."

I couldn't see the rest of HOW DO YOU BECOME BEAUTIFUL? on Faiza's sweatshirt with her body bent over the text she was reading aloud. When she straightened up, I was able to read MEET A RICH MAN. She asked the meaning of the expression "*avoir le cafard*" that ended the excerpt. Primed for the storm, Sandra blasted the question before it was half-asked.

"It's when a person has gloomy thoughts and all. Zample when a person feels lonely and all."

"But why do they say '*cafard*,' cockroach, for that? Do you know, Sandra?"

"Like I said, it's when you have these gloomy thoughts and all."

"Yes, but why the expression '*cafard*,' and not something else? What's the connection between a cockroach and gloomy thoughts?"

The group was fixed on the question and straining toward the answer. Hinda-who-looks-like-somebody-I-can't-recall took up the assault.

"It's because roaches are black and black goes along with gloomy thoughts."

"Okay if that's it then why don't they say 'crow'?"

"Because crows are cheerful."

"And cockroaches are sad?"

"Sure, they're always having *'le cafard,'* they're always gloomy."

Sandra gave a thousand-volt laugh, no sooner fired up than switched off.

"Actually it's because roaches are little, they can't do anything, they're always having trouble. So they wish they were bigger, but they can't be and so they're disgusted."

"In that case you could say *'avoir le fourmi,'* because an ant isn't awfully big either."

The emerging rumble had made me raise my pitch. Mohammed Ali raised his to match,

"That's not true, m'sieur, in Morocco there are ants big like this, I swear, my aunt told me that."

There was room enough for a Doberman in the space between his two hands showing the size of Moroccan ants. Michael said that Mohammed's aunt probably ate those ants, and the offended nephew said Yeah your aunt she eats zebra shit, and the others shouted in disgust. Sandra yelled Damn, you see those lightning flashes? setting a fire in the classroom that the hammering rain itself could not douse. To do some dousing myself, I picked up the white folder that held the next day's practice final exam. Instant silence.

"In the French part of the exam, if you pay attention to the instructions, you can pile up points."

I paced the rows, a colonel inspecting the tidiness of the uniforms.

"Above all, between now and tomorrow, don't spend all night with your nose stuck in math review. Get some air instead. Think about something else. Anyhow, the night before for the next day doesn't ever help. The memory is set before that, by sleeping. At the most, glance through a couple of notebooks for reassurance, but the game is pretty much over already. What you can still do is pay attention to basic moves: get in on time, come even a little early to get to the right room and seat, be sure to bring all your things with you. And above all, get some good sleep. It's very important to get some good sleep. A good sleep is fifty percent of the job."

As soon as it was allowed, two-thirds of them stood up noisily. Their backpacks already zipped and ready to go for some time, they rushed at once toward my desk to hand in their nameless exam papers. Only Jie, Jiajia, Xiawen, Alexandre, and Liquiao were left, bent over their calculators, trying new combinations of figures on their pink draft sheets, ignoring the hallway hullabaloo of the liberated students. Then Alexandre left, too.

Angelique had already put on her thick jacket but on her way out she detoured past my desk, with Camille trailing a little behind.

"M'sieur that composition for after vacation I'm not gonna be turning it in."

"Oh? And why won't you be turning it in?"

"Because acshully I won't be here after."

"Oh? And why won't you be here?"

"Well because acshully I'm gonna be finishing ninth grade in a different school."

"Oh? And where you going?"

"To 94."

"Oh? And why you going over there?"

"Well because my new foster family lives over there."

"I see."

"So that's why it's not worth me doing the composition."

Camille was listening with a look of condolence. Whatever I'd say would be wrong.

"Well then, good luck for the rest of the year. I hope you'll go on into tenth."

"Thank you. Goodbye."

She moved off, harnessed by her backpack that hung down to mid-thigh and that I would never see again.

After two days of practice exams, they were in no mood to work. Privately applauding my own sensitivity, I proposed a free-expression period, with a couple of minutes beforehand to consider what they might want to tell the world if they had the chance.

Mohammed Ali volunteered to go first, then got up and perched on the platform. I had not pictured the process like that, but I withdrew to listen to him from the back of the room. His heavy fake gold chain gleamed against the white of his TIMBERLAND sweatshirt.

"Ladies and gentlemen today I would like to talk special to our friends from Mali who yesterday, alas, suffered a huge defeat. A huge defeat of 4-0, which they suffered at the hands of the great Morocco team. Ah well that's how it is, and we'll all pray that Morocco beats our Tunisian friends in the final. But I see that since their defeat the Malians are showing a poor attitude. Up till the semi-finals, they were calling themselves Africans, and now that they're out of the competition—defeated 4-0 by the great Morocco team—now that they're out of the competition they say they don't care anything about Africa, and that's not right."

The teasing grin never left his face, and his rapper hands, palms up in the air, accented each segment of the sentence.

"I won't mention any names but there are some people in this classroom who been acting like that, and to them I wanna say don't be sore losers, and keep on being Africans, even if you do have a very weak team. So I invite the Malians to support the great Morocco team in the grand finale that's coming Saturday against our Tunisian friends. I thank you."

Part of the class applauded. Spinning his cap on his fist,

Souleyman—to whom the speech was pointedly addressed—shook his head with the meaningful look of a person who plans to get even.

"You have the right to respond if you like, Souleyman," I said.

"I don't care, he can say anything he wants that bastard."

Imani, who had previously booked a free-talk slot, was already up on the platform.

"Can I go, m'sieur?"

"We're listening."

"Well then . . ."

She took a deep breath and an amused expression.

"Well, I like to say sorry because it's true four-to-nothing is kind of rough, but okay when you're the best you're the best, but anyhow still I'm sorry for the Malians, and I feel for them because a defeat like that must be rough to take. But us Moroccans we're very happy since yesterday, that's it, have a good vacation everybody."

twenty-seven

A guy in his seventies was smoking with no lips, his gaze set on the newspaper stuck up behind the copper bar where the uniformed server had put out a cup.

"You'll see, he's gonna get re-elected, the Spain guy."

"Goes to show war pays."

Outside, the unfolding daylight gave me a glimpse of the backs of Marie and Jean-Philippe passing by the Chinese butcher shop. As I turned the corner I saw them pushing open the massive wooden door. In the interior courtyard, four custodians with metal shovels were pushing the remains of muddy snow against the various walls. Jean-Philippe and Marie had just come into the staff room, where Valerie was riveted to her e-mail and Gilles to the jammed copy machine.

"Hey."

Julien came in, his face tanned except for around the eyes. Gilles's face was tanned except for the face.

"It gives me a pain coming back here, you cannot imagine."

"It's tough, huh?"

"No kidding."

Lina was dozing on her feet beneath the lady with the umbrella.

"Omigod it was good sleeping late."

"No kidding."

Dico hung back from climbing the stairs with the others.

"M'sieur could I change classes?"

"No."

"Why not? This one sucks."

"You're in it, that's why."

"So are you."

"Get going."

Most of the group was waiting outside the physics room. Frida was pouring out a story to a semicircle of girls drinking in every word.

"He calls me up he goes can I come over I'm in trouble. I go I'm not just some like backup you can't just . . ."

"Okay, let's go in."

Souleyman walked in with his hood up.

"Souleyman."

He turned toward me, saw me point to my head to connote his own, just waiting for the signal.

"The cap too, please."

I wrote the title of the novel they were to buy on the board, and below it the author's name.

"There, this is a French writer. Uh no, actually not, he's Belgian, but he mainly lived in France."

Hand raised, Dounia waited without impatience for me to call on her.

"Does that mean it's a translation?"

She was rather proud of the word translation, showed a certain satisfaction at having pronounced it.

"Well actually no, because you know the Belgians generally speak French. Almost half of them. There are the Walloons and then there are the—"

Khoumba sat up straight at the Flemish.

"I'm not buying the book."

I was speechless for a moment.

"What, you've found your tongue?"

"Just to say I'm not buying the book."

"And why not?"

"I dunno I'm not buying it that's all."

"Leave the room."

She immediately headed for the door, which put the justification ball in my court.

"Next time, you ask to speak when you want to attack someone."

She stopped short and faced me.

"Who'd I attack?"

Djibril, ADIDAS 3, decided the dispute by hissing her.

"Did you see that m'sieur, how he hissed me?"

"Get away, I never hissed you. Pfffh."

"Yes you did so hiss me.

"I din hiss you I don give a fuck about you. Pfffh."

"M'sieur you let him talk to me that way but I say about the book and I got to leave the room?"

I crossed my arms and assumed the look of a person who's had a good night's sleep and waits serenely for the fuss to be over. My tone unmasked my agitation.

"I don't give a damn about your dramas. I just want you to leave the room, and I don't want to hear how some book is too expensive from people who buy themselves kebabs for lunch every day."

She had her hand on the doorknob.

"I don't like kebabs."

The door slammed on the kebab.

I had certainly noticed Mariama gradually slump down in her seat, either demoralized or looking that way, which came to the same thing. Still, I put off asking about it because that would risk breaking through the miraculous calm of this late afternoon. She took the initiative herself as I stood looking over her neighbor's exercise paper.

"M'sieur can I talk to you after?"

"Yes yes, of course."

She waited for the bell and the subsequent flight of her co-disciples, and then approached my desk like a little girl who cannot find her way home. At her first word the tears beaded beneath her dark pupils.

"M'sieur . . ."

"Go ahead, speak—that's what I'm here for."

Her cheeks trembled under the weight of the imminent tears.

"I'm lost."

A cellphone hung at her chest, and her eyes were fountains now.

"What do you mean, lost?"

"I don't understand anything."

"Understand anything about what?"

"All of it. I don't understand anything about what we're doing."

"In French class you don't always give me that impression."

She fumbled at the cellphone with one hand, and with the other wiped at the continuous flow of her tears.

"Sometimes I manage but mostly I don't understand anything."

She was standing, I was seated.

"You know, it's not so serious not to understand everything. No one understands everything, you know. Even me sometimes—I only understand half of what I'm saying."

She didn't laugh.

"The thing is to do the best you can, and then see."

She wasn't crying now, and my voice was like a doctor reassuring a hypochondriac who's really sick.

"What you should do is think about your plans for next year. Are you doing that?"

She snuffled up the remains of her tears.

"Yes, I made an appointment with the guidance counselor."

"That's the most important thing. Making some good choices. Making good choices about what you'd like within what's possible. Right?"

She blew her nose loudly. I wouldn't have thought she realized that it was all over for her socially. She shrugged her shoulder into a backpack that seemed loaded with tombstones.

"But if I want to do a general academic program in *lycée* then I don't have to bother about choosing or anything, right?"

"Yes, but if it turns out you can't do that, it's a good idea to think ahead and look into a good vocational course."

"I don't want to do vocational."

"Yes, but in case."

"All right, thank you m'sieur."

Before giving the floor over to the guidance counselor, the principal wanted to do a brief review of the results on the practice *brevet* exam.

"Before giving the floor over to the guidance counselor, I'd like to do a brief review of the results on the practice *brevet* exam."

A few latecomer students tiptoed over to empty chairs, which were the majority and would remain so despite a gradual shift in the ratio.

"I must say I was a bit disappointed. You should understand that the practice exam isn't meant to discourage, it's meant to provide signposts. But this time there truly is reason to be discouraged. In math, for instance, it's very disturbing. There I believe it's a matter of blocks. Psychological blocks. Because otherwise I don't see the reason. You shouldn't panic at the sight of a math problem. You should stay calm, take the time to really read over the instructions. Often half the answer can be found in the instructions."

He paused for a moment, thought over his words, cleared his voice with a cough—the winter was unyielding.

"My own conviction is that repeating the ninth grade is not an option. There's a place for every one of you in *lycée*. It may be in general academic, in technology, in vocational—but there is a place."

I didn't follow the rest of his remarks. Two rows ahead of me I had just recognized the one-armed man—or anyhow the person I *called* that, because this time he had no limb missing. He followed every word of the preamble, occasionally nodding his chin in agreement. After a few minutes he buttoned up his overcoat, then looked deep into my brain before disappearing through the swinging doors. At the same moment, a white head appeared, then a suited body attached to it. The principal caught sight of it in the course of an automatic twist of his torso, smiled at it, waved it forward, and introduced it as the headmaster of a vocational high school in a neighboring district. Later, he would be feeding our kids who were going for advanced vocational diplomas into the institution he ran.

Jacqueline had panicked.

"I panicked, I panicked. When I looked back at the topic afterwards, I knew exactly how to handle it all, but with the sheet in front of me I completely lost it."

In her time, Danièle had panicked too.

"The *agregé* exam—that thing's a trap. You're out of the circuit, you've lost the habit."

For fear of doing miserably, Lina had kept putting off taking the teacher promotion exam year after year. She changed the subject.

"Oh lala, look at him, isn't he the hard worker!"

I acknowledged it with a dopey smile then concentrated on my scissors.

"Mariama is up to her old tricks."

That could only be Jean-Philippe, talking at me from behind. I turned, he was standing beneath the waterlilies painted in blue.

"Last Thursday she started up again making fun of the Chinese girls in your class."

"Ah?"

"She was making little noises like when you try to mimic Chinese people."

My scissors suspended, I turned sideways on my chair, and he bit off some of his licorice-stick nicotine substitute.

"She keeps doing it, since the beginning of the year she's been doing it."

"Yeah, yeah, I think I've noticed it too."

Geraldine came back from the stockroom with a carton full of plastic goblets.

"Anybody have change for five euros?"

Jean-Philippe lodged the licorice stick between his lips to pull a coin out of his jeans.

"Meantime, the Chinese girls aren't trying very hard either."

Geraldine freed the goblets from their cellophane wrapper.

At the end of the chapter, there's a kind of resurrection. Like Jesus's."

General indifference, except for Dounia, who had read the book and had told me there were too many descriptions.

"Maria, can you explain what a resurrection is?"

Mohammed, DISTRICT 500, answered instead.

"'S like when some player loses like three matches and all of a sudden he starts winning again."

"M'sieur you got that silver tooth for a long time now?"

Far left row, first seat, he was wearing his expression designed to annoy the entire solar system.

"I don't see what that has to do with the resurrection. It would be different if you at least knew what it is, but you don't."

"Sure I know."

"So?"

"I don't feel like saying."

"You know I'm putting together a file on you for permanent expulsion?"

"I don't give a shit about your file."

Bell rang, birds flew: Fortunée and Amar chased each other out accompanied by shouts from Souleyman, whose cap Djibril had snatched and passed to Kevin, who threw it behind the cupboard, and Souleyman said M'sieur my hat's back behind the closet.

"What do you want me to do about it?"

Khoumba took off with mouth firmly shut, Mariama was waiting for Dianka whose thumb was keyboarding on her cellphone, Mohammed was still in his seat writing down the lesson without understanding it, Alexandre waited for him, Souleyman was sliding an arm behind the cupboard with his face twisted and his cheek jammed against the wall, Frida was tracing a heart in the fog on the window, Dico came up to me.

"M'sieur how come teachers always trying to get revenge?"

"Who're you talking about?"

"Like when you tell me you keeping a file on me that's revenge."

"That's discipline, it's not the same thing."

True to form, he didn't look at me, stood tracing circles with one foot, each retort threatened to be the last.

"You taking revenge because you are so mad from when I answered you back in front of the class that's all."

"When a judge puts somebody in prison, that's not getting even, it's so society can function."

"You not a judge and you getting even that's all."

With that, he turned on his heel to the door, leaving me in a fury.

"M'sieur looka my hat it's all full of dirt that's not right."

"The best thing would be not to wear hats any more, I'd say."

He shoved it onto his skull and mumbled a rap, Nothin to build up nothin to break down whaduv I got left ceptin my joy.

I had asked six students who were getting individual help to list five unfamiliar words they'd come up against over the past week. One after the other, they set out a column on the board. Nassanaba wrote SIMULATE, OBJECT, STAMMER, STRAY, OVERSTEP.

"Only verbs?"

"That's no good?"

"No, it's fine."

Rather ugly Sofiane wrote: ACROBAT, APPROPRIATE, SUGGEST, DEMENTED, CONTRACEPTION. Mody: SIDEREAL, GALAXY, BIG BANG, COMET, SALSIFY. Katia: METAMORPHOSIS, FRATERNITY, STIMU-LATOR, MEGALOMANIA, FLASH-BACK. Yelli: DOWRY, USURER, RELATE, RAPACIOUS, INDICTMENT. Ming: AUSTRIAN, BRONZE, MERIDIONAL, MEGALOMANIA, BULK.

Taking the lists one by one, I asked if anyone knew some of the words the others had collected. None did, so I explained them, except for the word Austrian, which the non-Chinese all knew. Turning to Ming, I said that Austrian was actually pretty well known, but that all right it was really a small country, that people didn't care much about Austrians.

"But you do know the country called Austria, don't you, Ming?"

"No."

"Okay, well actually it's not worth straining your brain over it, because generally speaking it's a country of no importance in the world, and not even in Europe. Does anyone know of a famous Austrian?"

Not a hand raised—free pass.

"See, I told you. If a bomb wiped Austria right off the map, no one would even notice."

Seated alongside Mezut, who was sniveling for some reason, Salimata pointed to her watchless wrist to catch the attention of Abderhamman in the next row. He flattened his hands against an imaginary windowpane, one finger folded. I had slept badly, and I hesitated but then spoke without thinking:

"Salimata, if you want to know the time ask me."

She flushed in advance at her bold move:

"What time is it, please?"

Ndeye laughed, JAMAICAN SPIRIT across her green and yellow sweatshirt.

"It makes you laugh when your pal is insolent, Ndeye?"

"It's not her making me laugh, m'sieur."

With an involuntary glance she indicated Bien-Aimé, whose ballpoint had leaked onto his 89 jacket.

"M'sieur could I ask somebody for a handkerchief?"

"Who's got a handkerchief for Bien-Aimé?"

Fayad stood up to pass along the Kleenex that Ming held out into the aisle.

"You ask permission before you stand up, Fayad." He sat back down.

"Kin I get up, m'sieur?"

"Now yes, okay."

As he went, he tripped on Tarek's backpack and caught himself by leaning onto Indira's shoulder. Abdoulaye, who never missed a chance to sit beside her, said,

"Oh that perv he'll use anything to touch—"

Alyssa did not laugh along with the rest of them because something was bothering her.

"M'sieur why do they say imperfect of the indicative—why do they say 'of the indicative'?"

"I turn the question back to you—why do they?"

This time her pencil was not to survive the attack by her canines.

"Okay, you others, did you hear the question? Why 'of the indicative'? Yes Bien-Aimé, we're listening."

"M'sieur, can I go to the bathroom?"

"Go to the bathroom, go, get it over with. All right, somebody else? Why 'of the indicative'?"

On his way back to his seat Fayad had swiped a white-out pen from Hadia in her bandana headdress, and now he was making it drip onto Demba's paper.

"All right then: if they specify 'of the indicative' it's so it won't be confused with some other imperfect—and what imperfect is that?"

Abderhamman took off his watch and set it before him, leaning against his pencil case, then said,

"Imperfect of the subjunctive."

"Good. And what is the imperfect of the subjunctive?"

They didn't know. I explained. I wrote "*il faut que j'aille,*" and then "*il fallait que j'allasse.*" They all laughed,

"Oh lala, old-timey."

"All right, it's true that these days people don't care much about the imperfect of the subjective. You'll come across it in books, and even then not very often. In spoken language, no one uses it. Except very snobby people."

Hadia in her bandana asked,

"What's snobby?"

"It's the kind of people, you know, who have fancy stuck-up ways."

For lack of the right words, I mimicked them, pursing my lips, arching my back and stretching my neck. "You get it, or not?"

The question mark running across Alyssa's face became an arrow determined to split the heavens.

"That look! If we did that everybody would go, Omigod what they doing there? They sick or what?"

Souleyman walked in with his hood up.

"Souleyman."

He turned to me, saw me point at my head to indicate his. Imitated me literally.

"The cap too, please."

Meanwhile, Michael had apparently decided on his own to break off his partnership with Hakim by sitting alone at the back of the room.

"Michael I totally approve of your move, whose purpose, I am sure, is to do better work. Am I mistaken?"

"No m'sieur."

The class guffawed. At the desk in front of him, Hinda lowered her head in embarrassment, hiding her face that looks like I can't think who.

"No other motive, are we in agreement?"

"Yes, yes. It's so I'll quit gabbing."

Hinda had still not raised her head.

"For instance you're not going to pester Hinda, do we agree?"

He said Noo! in a tone of obvious fact, stretching out the vowel. Hinda stared at her nails. Sandra was plugged in to her own internal electric plant.

"M'sieur can we talk about the attacks?"

"What do you want to say?"

"They keep saying it's the Islamists, and really nobody even knows."

"It's pretty likely, though, isn't it?"

Mohammed Ali and Soumaya instantly leapt onto the barricades, their enraged cries intertwining.

"Why they saying it's the Islamists? Long as there's no proofs nobody knows they should just shut up that's all, iss not right."

"And so? What difference does it make?"

Mohammed Ali broke away from the vindictive squad.

"The difference is they don't know that's all."

Soumaya caught up.

"Even September eleventh they didn't know anything either."

Imani joined the race.

"I was glad about September eleventh."

And I was glad of the chance to pull that apart.

"Three thousand people dead and you're glad?"

Mohammed Ali started up again.

"Well m'sieur what about all the dead people the Americans are making in Palestine and all."

"Yes, agreed, but we can't stay stuck forever in the spiral of vengeance."

"But if the Americans they kill Muslims, 's natural Muslims are gonna fight back."

"By killing just anybody?"

Big noisy argument, but now I wasn't listening to anyone but myself.

"Look, say I'm Pepita, I'm twenty-four years old, I live on the outskirts of Madrid. I have two little children, I work in Madrid, so I get up at six in the morning to take the train into town. And it also so happens that last year I went on a protest march against the Iraq war, and against my government being an ally of the Americans in the illegal invasion of a country. Okay, so like I do every morning, I climb on board my suburban train, I'm thinking about all that, about my children, about the war and all that, and then Boom, I'm dead."

Like a spell, my words brought on a silence. Intoxicated by this triumph, I went on,

"It's like me. As it happens I'm a little like Pepita, I take the metro in the morning, I actually take three different trains to get here, and it also happens that I am against the law about head-scarves. Now apparently there are some folks who want to set off bombs to protest that law. So there you are, I'm going to die, blown up over a law that I don't support. Nice, huh?"

The spell went on still. In the silence, Sandra's voice resonated strangely. Extraordinarily tender. Unplugged. Acoustic.

"What's that mean, support?"

"Support means to agree with."

"Yes but if the French people don't *say* they don't agree, it's like they do agree. Did you say that—did you tell people—that you don't agree?"

"A little."

"A little means nobody heard you and so there you are, the Islamists can't know it."

"As your head teacher I'll be escorting you to the museum Thursday. It goes without saying that you should write that trip down in your home-note booklet and get your parents to sign off on it."

LOVE ME TENDER sewn onto her pullover, Frida frowned intelligent eyebrows.

"What is it, Frida?"

"M'sieur I didn't understand what you said."

"But it's simple: there's a class trip."

"But you said some other thing I didn't understand."

"All I said was there would be a museum trip."

"But you said like, He won't say, or something."

"It goes without saying?"

"That's it."

"It goes without saying—that means it's not worth the trouble to say a thing, it's so obvious."

She grimaced, as if smelling some unpleasant odor.

"That's weird."

"It's weird, but it just means that obviously you all have to let your parents know."

On the left, first row: Dico never disappoints.

"Can we bring some friends?"

Pretend not to have heard.

"M'sieur can we bring friends?"

"What did I tell you before class?"

"I'm just asking, that's all."

I had told him: First wrong move, out you go.

"But it's just, like, a question is all."

"Okay, out."

He knew the way, and ten seconds after the door closed behind him, he started making mouth noises through the ventilator opening. Charging into the hall, I caught him in the act.

"Okay that's it—follow me to the office."

He trailed me down the stairs, setting between us a no-man's-zone three yards wide which became wider still in the courtyard. At the doorway to the office, I pushed back to move him ahead.

"You don't touch me, why you touching me?"

"Move ahead and keep quiet."

The principal was busy at his computer. He turned around at my unannounced greeting, which I made as lilting as could be.

"I'm terribly sorry to bother you again but Dico is stirring up a new crisis."

"All right, I'll take care of it."

He shot a look into Dico's eyes from below.

"Sit down."

Dico burrowed into the tufted chair. I was no longer looking at him.

"If he doesn't write me an apology, I won't take him back tomorrow. At the end of term I'm going to ask for an expulsion."

"In that case, you'll have to make out an incident report."

"Very well, I'll give it to you at noon today. I'm really sorry."

The dragon on Leopold's sweatshirt would spit fire if anyone annoyed him.

"Hey, you don't look too good."

Gray complexion, shadows under the eyes, anarchic whiskers around the mouth, sideburns uneven, Gilles did in fact not look too good.

"It shows that much?"

"Well yeah, really."

Gray skin.

"I had some kind of attack Friday."

"Oh no?"

Shadows under eyes.

"I was standing at the board, and suddenly I couldn't stand up. I just managed to grab onto the desk."

"The kids help you?"

Anarchic whickers.

"Yeah, they came and held me up under the arms so I could go sit down."

"You should have asked for leave."

Around the mouth.

"I don't know, that bothers me. Even now, being here all the time, we still get such miserable scores on the practice *brevet* exam."

"You can't feel obligated."

Uneven sideburns.

"On top of that, I just opened my administrative evaluation, that got me down completely."

Claude was rubbing a fifty-centime coin against his thigh to exorcise its inefficacy. He slipped it into the machine as delicately as if he were trying not to wake it up, and it reappeared out the bottom.

"Shit."

Gilles automatically handed him another fifty-centime coin.

"I'm sorry but it's like here you are, you come in, you try to do some minimum of a job, and those people upstairs who have no idea what you do, they lay some shit score on you, it's really depressing."

Sitting over in the lounge corner, Sylvie was pregnant.

"I think Moussa is depressive."

Rachel had three children, one a girl.

"Do you?"

"Yeah. In my class he sleeps all the time."

Bastien wasn't pregnant because he was a man.

"You know it's pretty natural in a way, his father was in a motorcycle accident last year. He had a real hard time. Six months in the hospital, something like that. He's in a wheelchair now."

"Oh yes, Moussa wrote me a paper on the handicapped."

To save face, Claude was taking the coffee machine apart.

"Anybody got ten centimes?"

Sylvie had the coin, but not the inclination to give it. Bastien was still set on his idea as well as on his cookie.

"No, but, imagine, the father going 200 kilometers an hour on his bike and smack into the wall, of course the kid's gonna be in bad shape."

"That's why I think he's depressive."

Having put the machine back together, Claude was thinking about another drink and gave Gilles back his coin.

"Hey, you don't look too good."

Rachel came over to the lockers from which I had just pulled a half-sheet of paper that smelled of oranges.

"Do you remember that we're going to the museum the day after tomorrow?"

"Yes, sure."

> Monsieur I apologize for disrupting your class and I
> ask you to please forgive me. I promise to make efforts
> in my work and in my behavior.
> Dico.

"What's that?"

Bastien didn't give a damn what it was, he just wanted to talk. I handed him the half sheet. A few crumbs from his cookie fell onto it, then, sliding across the large squares, dropped through the void to land soundlessly on the linoleum.

Xiawen was wearing a necklace of small crosses. I began counting them off but was immediately interrupted by their owner's leaning toward her neighbor, Liquiao, to snatch the French-Chinese dictionary, which she leafed through quickly with one finger, as a professional would a pile of banknotes. I woke up.

"Okay, you've had enough time to think. I want two reasons why it's uncomfortable to talk about your lives."

Three hands raised.

"Only three with an idea? Not bad out of twenty-five. What does that make, three out of twenty-five?"

Three hands lowered, two raised. Two left.

"Yes, Jihad?"

"Uh, a quarter."

"That's right, you're absolutely correct, three times four makes twenty-five—well forget it. Two reasons why it's awkward to tell about your life? I'm listening."

Three hands raised.

"Yes, Maria?"

JAMAICA on her sweatshirt.

"Because it could upset your parents."

"Yes, that's so. And more generally, all the people close to you, or all the people involved. What else? Dounia?"

Hair in a black bandana.

"It doesn't necessarily make any money."

"Yes, that's pretty much true, but actually that has no direct connection with the topic. Frida, we're listening."

Hair in a red bandana.

"I don't know if this is right."

"We're listening."

"But I don't know if it's right."

"We're listening."

"Well, because you feel embarrassed, too."

"Ah, explain that to me."

"I don't know how to explain. Like, if sometimes you did something you feel ashamed about it."

"Very good. Shame—that's interesting. We've all done something we're ashamed of. Give me some examples of things a person could feel ashamed of."

They came up with some easily, but they sniggered rather than speaking out openly.

"I'm not necessarily asking for a memory of your own. Give me some things in general that could make a person feel ashamed."

They exhanged meaningful looks and held their noses as if assailed by evil-smelling recollections.

"OK then, if no one wants to talk, I'll tell you something myself."

Golden silence.

"I was about twelve, I think, and at the time I didn't know much, at least about certain things, some yes but others not, and every morning a few of us would get together in the courtyard, three girls and two boys. We were like a little club, the kind of group that takes shape in the courtyards of apartment buildings, you know, and of the three girls there was one I would have loved to fool around with, but actually that part of it doesn't matter. Anyhow, one morning I come out and she's not there, and one of the other girls says of course not, she'd called her up the day before and the girl said she had a stomachache, and then the other boy says oh, she has her period? and the girl says you got it, and me, I say what's a period? and the two of them look at each other like, who is this bozo? And so that's my story, whenever I think back on it I shiver with shame. Even though I really shouldn't. There's nothing shameful about it."

The lecturer moved along ahead of the group by a few yards, then stopped beside a case built of wood and metal, with mirrored trusses that reflected back and forth endlessly.

"Here's a piece called 'Infinity Made Matter.' What does that title make you think of?"

Neither those who had reached the chest first nor the later arrivals had an answer.

"Doesn't that expression seem a little bizarre, 'Infinity Made Matter'?"

Nor did those arriving only now.

"You feel those two words go well together—'infinity' and 'matter'?"

Without understanding, Jihad did understand that her tone meant No, and he whispered a No that the lecturer took for a signal she could go on.

"No, of course not, because the material world is by definition finite, the opposite of infinite. Infinity, on the other hand, is associated with the spiritual, with what is not material."

Between the contemporary walls resounded her voice.

"So here this artist is bringing together the two ideas in the one title, and even more so in a single object. How does he do that?"

Nor did Djibril, who had wandered off and was just rejoining us.

"Look carefully at the surfaces. What are they made of?"

Jihad, who was looking at himself in them, said,

"Mirrors."

"Very good—they're made of mirrors, and that's how the artist constructs the infinite through matter, in matter, inside matter."

Beneath her show of gravity, Sandra was smiling.

"M'sieur, you have Souleyman?"

"In the 9-A, yes. You find that funny?"

"You know what he did to Hinda?"

I indicated No by creasing my brow. Her upturned hands gripped the edge of my desk.

"You didn't hear?"

"Well no."

"He made her bleed like crazy."

"On purpose?"

"Well sure. He wanted to get even because he thought Hinda was making fun of him, when she really wasn't."

The others were taking their time to sit down, opening the windows with complaints that the room stank. And in fact Hinda was not there. I raised my voice so Sandra could hear me.

"So how did he make her bleed?"

"He cut her on this place here."

Pointing between the temple and the eye socket.

"The brow?"

"Yeah, there."

She let a few internal functions go quiescent but she was seething to set them going again.

"Listen, it sounds like it's fairly serious, what happened, so I don't understand why you're smiling."

"I'm not smiling."

"Yes, you're smiling."

"No, I'm not smiling."

"A good fight makes a nice little distraction in school, huh?"

She set one foot on the platform, then put it back on the floor, moves that uncovered and then masked her navel.

"Omigod there was blood everywhere it was like horrible to see, I swear on my life."

"See, there you go—you're laughing."

"Honest, it was horrible."

"OK, go sit down."

The period passed, I asked Why write your life, they said it was to show off. I'd slept badly, I said The lives of the guys who write them are not necessarily so glorious, they said They can lie and fake things, I said That's for sure, they said Anyhow who cares if they tell us about their lives, I said It's interesting because maybe their lives are a little like our own and even if they're not like ours exactly that's even more interesting, it's about finding out about life in general, actually telling about our own life is just that—telling about life, you see what I mean? They said But what can you do with all that? and vanished at the sound of the bell like a flight of sparrows drawn by more nourishing crumbs somewhere else. Sandra detoured past my desk.

"M'sieur it's true what I told you before."

"I believe you, but stop smiling."

"I'm not smiling. Souleyman—he's gonna get a Disciplinary Council hearing."

"Oh?"

"Well yeah, acourse."

Chantal, Jean Philippe, Luc, Rachel and Valerie were ranged around the oval table for a class council on grades. As head teacher, Chantal ran the discussion.

"Sonia: what do you all think about her?"

"Not much."

"She never smiles. It's weird."

"My opinion—it's mainly shyness."

"Yes but last year she wasn't like that, she smiled."

"What do I put down for general evaluation?"

"Not so hot."

"I put 'Average overall'?"

"Yeah."

"OK. Youssef?"

"Omigod, that one."

"What's he like in your class?"

"He's all right."

"What about yours?"

"Marginal."

"No, in mine he does okay."

"Gotta keep him separate, that's all."

"In tutoring he's a drag."

"So in general, among us all who exactly is he a problem for?"

"Me."

"Me."

"Yeah, he irritates me too."

"Unless you tell him enough is enough now, he just won't shut up."

"So—unruly?"

"That's it—unruly."

"OK, fine—unruly student, must correct his behavior. Going on to Aghilès."

"Omigod, that one."

"Is he aggressive!"

"I put down 'Aggressive student'?"

"That's a little strong, aggressive."

"We can't say that? If he's aggressive we've got to put aggressive, otherwise . . ."

"No, what you can put is 'Sometimes shows aggressive tendencies.'"

"Okay, fine, I'll put that. And onward—Yann next."

"Omigod, that one."

"No, really, he gabs a little less recently."

"Sure he does—he gabs a little less because he knows the grade meeting is coming up, that's all."

"You think so?"

"I mean really."

"So I'm putting, 'Talks too much.' And his work?"

"What work?"

"He does absolutely nothing."

"The work's as minimal as his size, is all you have to put."

"You know what the other kids call him?"

"No, what?"

"Mimi Mathy."

"Who's Mimathy?"

"Kinda funny, have to say."

"And true."

"Who's Mimathy?"

"A dwarf actress."

"Oh, I get it."

"Nassim's next."

"Omigod, that one."

"He's by far the worst."

"I put down 'Constant talking'?"

"He's always jumping around."

"Constant talking?"

"Talking and jumping around."

"But has he made some progress anyhow?"

"Not even. Too much jumping around."

"Up a half point in my class."

"Put 'talking and jumping around and no progress.'"

"What I can say is 'He talks too much and jumps around and could do better work.'"

"No, gotta say something more drastic than, 'Could do better work.'"

"To me, I find he throws the whole class off, that guy."

"Well in fact—what about the class as a whole, what do I put?"

"Too talkative."

"Yes, that's mainly it, too talkative."

"So you all agree on saying the class doesn't work hard enough and talks too much?"

Rather ugly, Sofiane was slow to leave the classroom. I finally let Arthur and Gibran come in for the next period. They both shrugged their backpacks onto the table, laughing about something or other. As she passed the trash basket, Sofiane tossed in a leaky ballpoint pen, and after she turned away I bent down to retrieve it. I wiped it clean by rolling it in a half sheet of paper, I tried it, it didn't work, and I put it back in the trash. The room filled up at the drowsy early-week pace. Hinda's seat would stay unfilled,

Hakim was whistling the *Marseillaise*, Arthur had not yet pulled off his parka, neither had Gibran.

"You know who won yesterday?"

Arthur didn't know, Gibran looked up at me in front.

"M'sieur, who won yesterday?"

"Won what?"

"The political thing."

"The Left."

Arthur hadn't taken anything out of his pack, neither had Gibran.

"And is that good?

"That's for each person to decide. What matters is the principle of the vote."

They smiled.

"Yes but for us, we don't understand anything about it."

"It's already a good thing to be talking about it."

Sandra hurtled into the room, a train without rails.

"Talking about what, m'sieur?"

"Take your seat, calm down, and I'll tell you."

She sat, calmed down, I told her. Instantly her internal power plant started up, and she told how she had watched the election returns with her father, it was so great, and on top of that there were no sex scenes, and at the next break Gilles was pale.

"We're already tired enough as it is, and then they swipe an extra hour of sleep from us."

Elise agreed.

"It's just one more bullshit thing."

Hinda was back. Setting the attendance sheet on her desk, I saw the stitches in her brow.

"Actually it's very cute, that little wound."

She let loose her smile, multiplying by seven the sparkle in her eyes and the likelihood of springtime.

"You think?"

"Oh yes. No lie."

"Thank you."

She looked like somebody, I can't remember who.

"Feeling better, at least?"

Another smile from the spring-summer collection.

"Yes, yes, I'm fine."

Michael stood and came up front.

"M'sieur, we copying down the assignment or we do it right away?"

"But you can't get up and move around like that, no. This isn't kindergarten, people don't just move around like that."

"'Scuse me, m'sieur."

With his eyes still on me, he dropped a folded bit of paper near Hinda, who grasped it furtively. I decided to have seen nothing and then harangued the company at large.

"Don't waste any time getting started, you only have an hour."

Imani raised his hand.

"We gotta tell a real memory?"

"Yes. Or at least something plausible. You know what that means, plausible?"

"It means saying just anything."

"No, that's 'im-plausible.' Plausible is the opposite, it's when a thing really could have happened."

"Clothes, for instance. Basically, why do we wear clothes? To keep warm, and then also out of modesty. But humans very soon added a third motive for dressing, which is to look good, to have their clothes suit their taste, or their personality, or the image they want to project. And for instance, what do we call the great dressmakers, or the people who invent clothes? They're called stylists, or designers. Which is to say that wanting to look good in your clothes means paying attention to style. Ndeye be quiet. Generally speaking, *style* is whatever is not strictly useful, functional. Well, the same thing is true for language. I can say something just to transmit information—for instance, that I was born in France. But I can say the same thing with style—for instance, I can say I was born in the land of cheeses, or in the land of the Rights of Man. There I'm doing style—bad style, but style. And for that I use a certain procedure, and this procedure has a name. Ndeye what did I just say? For instance, when I go to the skating rink, I could be happy just circling around on the ice, the way we all do when we're not champions. But what do champions do? They do figure eights, triple-flips and all that—Ndeye, this is the last time. To say 'the land of the Rights of Man' instead of just 'France,' that's called using a stylistic device, and there are many such devices of style. That one is called 'paraphrase.' But we know lots of others. What others do we know?"

Mezut had been crying for some reason at the start of the period. "Verbs."

"Please, Mezut, really. You do know that a verb is not a figure of speech. A verb is a verb. I mean really."

Alyssa knew the answer but preferred questions.

"Why do the French say that they're the land of the Rights of Man?"

"Because that's just what people say."

Bien-Aimé, 67 on his shirt, came to my rescue.

"M'sieur, you go to the skating rink?"

"Don't you?"

"That's really sad, m'sieur."

The ringing bell and the flying sparrows left behind Abdoulaye, who wanted to talk *tête-à-tête.*

"M'sieur, as class delegate I have something to tell you."

"Oh?"

"There's a couple of students who've asked me to pass something on to you."

I thought/hoped they would be asking me to take them again for the next year in ninth grade.

"It's about the class council."

"I'm listening."

He was calm, without fuss, bearing the great elegance of a finely-bred hoodlum in his white sweatshirt with black stripes.

"They feel like you ride them too much."

"Ah?"

"Yeah, there are some kids in class discussion period were saying you ride them too much. They want me to report that at the class council."

"But who says that? I mean, I'm not asking for names, but how many people say that?"

"I don't know, a few."

"Not a majority, though?"

"No, a few."

"All right."

"Goodbye, m'sieur."

"Goodbye."

"I'm sick and tired of these circuses. I can't look at them anymore, don't want to look at them anymore. They put me through hell, I can't do it, I can't stand them anymore, I can't do it, I can't, they don't know a goddamn thing and when you try to teach them something they look at you like you're a chair, but fine, let them stay in their shit, let 'em stay there, I'm not gonna chase after them, I've done what I was supposed to do, I've tried to pull them out but they don't want it, that's all, can't do anything about that, shit I can't look at them anymore, I'm gonna kill one of 'em for sure, they're absolutely so low, so dishonest, always looking to make trouble, but go ahead guys, go ahead stay right there in your crap neighborhood, your whole life you're gonna stay there and that's perfect, but on top of that they're just fine with it those assholes, they're satisfied to stay there those clowns, anyhow I'm gonna go see the principal and I'm gonna tell him that I'm not taking the 9-bs anymore from now on for the rest of the year, so they'll have two months less of physics. You think they care? they haven't done a second of physics this whole year, not a single second did they do, so look, two more lousy months of shit are not gonna change things, they're not gonna get to work now, not when they're half in heat, yelping like that in the courtyard and even in class, it's complete madness I tell you, they're like animals, I swear I never saw anything like it, I can't stand it anymore, it's not just the ninth-graders I'm gonna say I won't take anymore, it's everyone, that's right, I'm going to go see the principal and I'm gonna tell him I'm not taking any more students at all for the rest of the year or I swear I'll wind up killing one of them, he'll be mad, the principal, but it's practically a safety measure I swear to you, has anybody got a kleenex?"

To let in a little fresh air, the principal asked us to leave open the door to the study hall, which had been reconfigured for the occasion.

"Today we have come together because Souleyman has been summoned to appear at a Disciplinary Council."

The principal sat alone on the side opposite that of Souleyman, who was flanked by the two student delegates.

"I seriously emphasize the fact that, without wishing to anticipate the decision that will be taken, any penalty will have educational value. If the Disciplinary Council should today ask for permanent expulsion, it will be in order to give Souleyman the chance to make himself over elsewhere. It will be doing him a favor to remind him of the rules."

We reviewed the incident. Each person said what he thought—that it was inadmissible. That it was a pity but inadmissible. The school doctor wanted to explain that the brow was known to be a fragile area, and that the amount of blood shed was not an indication of a violent blow. Danièle said Still, three stitches. A large cross in false gold at her neck, the educator reported that she had often known Souleyman to exhibit a certain ethic, a certain moral rectitude.

Invited to respond in the absence of his mother, Souleyman said he had nothing to say, only that he had not meant to make Hinda bleed. He was asked to leave the room to allow us to deliberate. Red REDSKIN letters surrounded an Indian feather headdress on the back of his jacket.

We voted for permanent expulsion.

I had begun the class discussion period by asking them to express their grievances, then explained what grievances are, then said that they could also ask their Class Council delegates to express a general satisfaction, then explained overall or general as different from local or particular, then mentioned as if to myself my own strong preference for the latter. Then didn't know what else to say, looked at the time on Huang's ridiculously huge watch, and with enormous relief saw Jiajia raise her hand by some Olympian effort.

"Yes, Jiajia?"

"You have finish talk?"

That was said with a good many gestures meant to hoist her closer to her non-mother tongue.

"You're asking if I have more to say?"

"Yes that is it, yes."

For Jiajia to force herself into oral mode in public, her question must be truly important.

"No, I've finished, please go ahead."

The class was hanging on this rare moment and on Jiajia's lips. Laboriously, she explained she had had enough of the way certain students, anyhow one in particular she would not name, were always giving her a hard time. The others laughed knowingly: it was clear she meant Mariama, who pointed to herself.

"M'sieur that's not balanced like that."

She turned to Jiajia and took on the stance of a rapper, forearms waving, palms slicing the air, hostile contempt drawing down the corners of her mouth.

"Really, no, you got something to say to me you come see me and we talk about it but you don't go through the teacher like that no way."

Their boredom gone, the class was delighted. In vain I called for hands to be raised before speaking, warned that those who wanted to speak could do so only on condition of raising a hand, reminded that unless a person raised a hand nobody would get to speak. Jiajia and Mariama went at each other without any mediation from me. In her excitement, Jiajia became less and less clear. Mariama reproached her and the other three Chinese girls for keeping to themselves, making up a separate gang of four, Jiajia said that was her business, that she'd hang out with whoever she wanted, that she didn't reproach Mariama for being fat. Omigod I thought.

"No, Jiajia, no insults."

Mariama was scowling like Obelix, but I glimpsed a gap of silence. From Maria, sitting patiently with her hand up, I hoped for some definitive peacemaking.

"Yes, Maria, we're listening. Everyone, listen to Maria please. Maria raised her hand, therefore she may speak."

"M'sieur it is the truth they keep to themselves. Once I was in the bus and I asked Jie if she was gonna go out with Alexandre or something like that, because we see them talking together. Well she goes no I can't he's not my race."

Jiajia looked like she would have strangled her, would have gone on strangling her past death.

"But that is not problem of you, is problem of her."

The squabbling took off again stronger than ever. This time I waited till they all cancelled each other out, and then:

"What I think is that when we take in newcomers, well it's up to us to make twice the effort, because we're the ones who know things and they are just arriving, they're in the weaker position, they have to learn everything. With you, your parents were once in the same position that the Asian immigrants are in now and I'm sure they would have appreciated it if the people who'd already been here for a long time—people like me, say—went to some effort to welcome them, twice the effort the newcomers could make."

So saying, I was *moved* by my words, from the verb "to feel moved, *s'émouvoir*." The students hesitated between sarcasm and support. Khoumba would have had some nice things to say on the subject, but instead it was Dounia who spoke up.

"And so people who just come from the bled, from their village in Algeria, three years ago—what do they do, m'sieur? They sposed to help people, or do other people help them?"

"You know some people like that?"

"Me and my big brother."

"The people who are already here should make the effort, that's what I think."

Boubacar's lovely gaze asked for my assenting glance before speaking.

"M'sieur, it's hard though."

"Why's it hard?"

"Well, it's hard because like sometimes they don't speak French so well."

The pastry cook called Veronica, The pastry cook called her, *Le pâtissier l'a appelée.*

"Bamoussa, why do we put a double 'e' at the end of the verb?"

"Because Veronica is a girl."

"Right, but there's more."

Emboldened by the first question, he panicked at the second. Which was of no concern at all to Djibil, otherwise preoccupied as he was.

"M'sieur why in those examples they always say Veronica and never, I dunno, Fatima or something?"

"Veronica's a pretty name, isn't it? Veronica Jeannot was pretty."

"What?"

Born August 15, 1988 (too recently to know the actress), Mohammed was quick to mix in. His SWADE headband caught no sweat as he said,

"Fatima's pretty too. Thass my grandma's name, m'sieur. She makes cakes, m'sieur, I swear on my life they're the best cakes in the whole Maghreb."

"In that case, whoever wants to put Fatima put Fatima. You can even put Brigitte or Naomi or Robert, all I care about is just that you put the double *e* at the end of the participle."

Bamoussa was utterly shocked.

"But m'sieur if it's Robert that don't take two e's, cause it's a boy."

"Oh, excuse me, yes of course, you've got me all mixed up with your goings-on. So then, you can put Fatima, Brigitte, Naomi, but not Robert. What's the matter, Hakim?"

"Can we put Delphine?"

"No, not Delphine."

The sky fell in.

"But why?"

"Because Delphine is simply not permitted. In my class, there will never be any mention of a Delphine, or it'll be over my dead body."

I was rushing to the coffee machine and someone called me, it was Alyssa in a navy blue Timberland jacket with white bands. Alyssa, whose class I had just released two minutes early for the sake of the coffee I was running toward at the moment she called me in her navy blue Timberland jacket with white bands.

"M'sieur, I wanted to ask you, what's a semicolon?"

Coffee with no sugar, strong enough to set the tastebuds screaming.

"Look you know very well what a semicolon is. It's a dot over a comma."

"I'm asking how you use it. You're so stupid sometimes m'sieur."

No sugar, very hot.

"I've already explained how you use it."

"Yes, but I didn't understand."

Really steaming.

"Okay, it's less strong than a period and stronger than a comma, that's it."

"Well, okay but when do you use it?"

"Alyssa, I'm very sorry but I have to meet with a parent, we'll talk about this some other time."

"When?"

Three yards farther along, a nuclear plant threatening to explode and irradiate the capital, Sandra fidgeted, disregarded her breasts bouncing under her T-shirt, dropped and lifted the hem of her black jacket with yellow bands, quizzed the girls, provoked the boys, ran to meet Michael and Hinda who had gone off by themselves for a while and were now returning to the massed troops. The former was weeping and drawing away from the latter, who looked like somebody or other and had obviously just dumped him. Sandra folded Michael in her arms, saying No no, don't cry. Hinda restrained a smile, thus was not smiling. The weather was gloomy, some day the sun would pierce the dark of the interior courtyard and I'd take my coffee short.

"Next is Mezut."

The U gave one unanimous sigh. Lina spoke for the rest.

"What are we going to do with him?"

The unanimous U mutely gave no answer to what was not really a question.

"And he's not well, besides."

"Yes, he cries sometimes."

Serge the dean knew some things he was not permitted to tell.

"I think there are some little violence issues with the papa. The mother has already lodged complaints for herself and I wonder whether the boy might not have undergone some of it as well."

The principal did not let the icy silence spread.

"What is he asking for?"

"A general academic program."

The guidance counselor interrupted the unanimous astonishment.

"Obviously, when he says that, he doesn't realize—it's up to us to find him a situation more suited to his abilities. An apprenticeship, something like that."

"The problem is that he'd like to do a business program."

"He could take a business program right here in the courtyard during recess."

A self-satisfied snort of laughter from Julien, the author of the joke. Shamefaced laughter from his audience except for the principal who sent the ball back to the guidance counselor.

"There's room for everyone in tenth grade. Is there such a thing as an apprenticeship in business?"

"Oh yes, it's called a Business Apprenticeship. Roughly speaking it's stocking shelves in a supermarket, wonderful."

She said Wonderful and indicated the opposite by her grimace. The principal said it was something at least, and that Mezut should be helped to fill out his application, and that as to the rest, well it was terribly sad.

I hadn't been warned a transfer student was coming in, and he didn't introduce himself. He settled in at the rear left, in the seat vacated by Souleyman. I beckoned him to come up to my desk, MAFIA LAW on his long-sleeved polo shirt.

"Write out a sheet with your name, the school you're coming from, and your address, all right?"

I raised my voice to get the attention of the twenty-four others, as noisy as if they were arguing over three chairs.

"I'd like those who are still standing to sit down."

"They're not gonna do the opposite."

Mohammed Ali murmured that. I smiled sourly and squinted to imply, That's smart.

"Take out a sheet and write at the top, in capital letters, 'Correction review of the composition about an early childhood memory.'"

I turned back their papers. Sheng got only a fifteen. Gibran turned off his laughter over something or other, and asked if the grade would count for the second trimester. I said yes, but that this wasn't the time to calculate his average, rather he should pull out a sheet and take down the corrections. Katia had no paper, she asked for a sheet from Faiza who'd colored her hair red and stood up to give it to her and as she passed Sophie snatched it away from her and handed it on to Soumaya who seeing Katia making off with her assignment pad in exchange called on me to arbitrate.

"M'sieur that's not right."

"I'm not a nursery school teacher."

Sandra, hooked up to the short-circuited electric grid, said that her big sister was a nursery school teacher. Hakim said Nobody gives a damn about your sister, and Sandra said You better keep an eye on yours cause she hangs out with pimps every night. Everyone having got back his paper, I read aloud Amel's essay, which described his jealousy at the birth of a little brother. Cranky over his score of five, Haj was muttering.

"If a person don't have nothing to tell about, what's he supposed to do?"

"I'm sure everybody's got something to tell."

He grumbled.

"Whaddya want me to tell?"

"If you thought about it I'm sure you'd come up with something."

He groused.

"I'm not gonna tell about what I do, school and all, it's dumb."

"But school can be very interesting."

He sulked.

"No, it's dumb."

The bell sent off twenty of them at once. Staying behind were Sandra who was singing and shaking her little potbelly, Hinda who looked like somebody or other only better, Soumaya, who was sprouting some springtime pimples, and the new kid, who handed me his information sheet. His name was Omar, he was seventeen, and he had a tutor.

"Did you write an autobiography with your French teacher from before?"

"I don't remember."

"But you do understand what that is, at least?"

"It's when people tell about their life and all."

"Why did you change schools, did you move?"

"I was expelled."

"Uh-huh. And this time you're going to do some real work?"

"Yes."

Wenwu and his father were seated at the other side of my desk. I turned the report card toward the father so we could read it together, then changed my mind. Scanning it alone, I spoke to Wenwu, who occasionally translated and most often did not. We were saying things to one another we'd often said before in private. When it came time to go, the father nodded his head. Smiling and joining his hands, Wenwu said goodbye first for his father, a second time for himself.

"Goodbye, Wenwu."

A woman passed them on her way in, and as she took a seat she introduced herself as Mezut's mother. Her handsome brow creased constantly.

"I just don't understand, you see. It's true, yes, for Mezut not to see his father is hard, and it's true he also has his family in Switzerland and in Turkey, too, who he never sees, but aside from that he has whatever he needs. It's also true that he didn't want to come to this school, he wanted to stay with his friends down in the twelfth, but when we moved I said it was out of the question for him to take the metro, so I signed him up here, and it's true it was a little hard for him, but I don't think that's what the problem is, the problem I think is in his head, sometimes I tell myself that."

"I understand."

"I think Mezut he is a depressive, you see, and I wonder if he should go see a psychologist or something, see, because I think it's in his head, see, I mean mostly he doesn't ever talk, he's a nice boy, even if he's having trouble he won't say so, he piles things up, and I get the feeling he's depressed, not depressed but not happy, and yet he's not seeing his father anymore so I don't understand."

"I understand. You should come back so we can talk about it."

The next woman was blond like her son, yet I didn't connect them.

"I'm Kevin's mom."

"Yes, of course I do remember, sit down please. I'm glad you came in because I have a lot of things to tell you."

She sat down. I showed her the report card, stopping my finger at the grade for math. She understood, he had always had trouble with figures, she was planning to ask his older brother to give him more help in the third trimester, and does Kevin eat in class?

"Eat in class—meaning what?"

"Chips, snacks, things like that."

"You're asking me whether Kevin eats chips in class?"

"Yes, that's what I wanted to find out."

"Listen, I don't see everything that goes on but I don't think so."

She didn't react to my answer.

"Because he's put on twenty-five pounds this year and I never see him eating, so I wondered where he could be getting it."

"I see."

"And yes, okay, I'm all by myself so I can't always be running after him looking over his shoulder, when I'm at the tollbooth the whole day is gone by the time I get home, so maybe that's when he eats, twenty-five pounds in a year, you realize?"

"Yes."

"If his father was around it's a sure thing that would never have happened, and actually when he goes to his father's house during vacation he does tend to get thinner, because his father takes him fishing in the canal and he's not hanging around the house after school, you know?"

"Yes."

"Going fishing, he adores that, well it depends, as long as he gets a little help and he hooks something, because when he doesn't he clams up for three days, okay that gives us a little rest, though it's not so much that he talks a lot that's the problem, it's more that sometimes he says things he shouldn't say, so then I tell him You know Kevin those are things people shouldn't say, and then he tells me Yes I know I won't say them again, and then the next day it starts up again him saying things you aren't supposed to say, and I tell him Listen if you ever say that kind of thing to a boss you'll see what he says, isn't that right what I'm saying?"

"Oh yes."

Habiba couldn't get over it.

"The whole book, every sentence starts with 'I remember'?"

"Yes, yes, the whole book."

Plugged into two power plants at once, Sandra spoke without asking permission.

"Could I read it m'sieur?"

"Certainly not."

I would rather not have smiled, but she was so upset that by baring a couple of teeth I let her understand that yes of course she could read it, that she would understand it and like it because she had a talent for life. Mohammed Ali tugged at the hood of Hakim, who had given up trying to stop him. In any case, there was no way Haj would ever read the whole of this sick guy's book.

"It reminds people of their own time long ago, that's why, but otherwise it's dumb."

I bounced back. Pedagogy, sensitivity.

"Now about those memories—they're generally about what period, would you say? Mohammed Ali, leave that hood alone and tell me instead what period do these memories date from?"

"I don't know. 1985, around then."

"Was television still only black and white in 1985?"

"*I* don't know."

"You don't know, but if you poked your brain around a little maybe you could know. And the rest of you people too. Things don't come to you just like that."

Things didn't come like that or any other way. Even to Zheng, always straining toward the light, it didn't come. I'd had a bad night's sleep.

"Still, there's one memory in there that ought to put a bug in your ear."

Hakim had just thrown back his hood to be done with it.

"What's that mean, m'sieur?"

"What does what mean?"

"That bug thing you said I dunno what."

"Oh, a bug in your ear—it means a kind of hint: something that can lead to the answer. There's one memory that ought to lead you to an answer, and Hakim, you have the right to take off your hood altogether, then Mohammed Ali won't be tempted."

No bug in any ear. I'd have to drop a clue. Pedagogy.

"For instance, the character says 'I remember Johnny Hallyday's first concert.' That doesn't tell you something?"

Haj was born September 13, 1989, and it told him nothing.

"We don know whatever it was the date he started."

"There's a way to find out, though."

"Yeah maybe but we don't care about that guy."

I was starting to get annoyed.

"Well I don't care either, what do you think of that?"

"It's your generation, though."

Now I was annoyed.

"Oh yeah? You think Johnny Hallyday is my generation?"

"I dunno. He's old."

"How old?"

"I dunno, fifty."

"And how old am I?"

"I dunno, but if you know what's his age that means you were born before."

"Yes, sure, in fact, Johnny Hallyday is my son."

I'll start over.

"You didn't see the posters last year, all over Paris?"

"What posters?"

"You live in Paris, don't you?"

"Yeah."

"And you never saw those posters—'Johnny celebrates his sixtieth'?"

"I don't give a damn about him."

I was annoyed. Pedagogy.

"Look, me neither, I don't give a damn, you know? It's just that I live in Paris and the posters were all over town. And if he's sixty years old, he must have started in the 1960s, since singers usually start their careers at about twenty. And so Johnny Hallyday's first concert you could guess was in the 1960s, right? Right, the rest of you?"

Vaguely right, the rest of them.

"Mohammed Ali, if you're in love with Hakim just kiss him on the mouth, but leave his hood alone, give us a break."

thirty

A guy thirty, thirty-five years old was smoking an unmelancholy cigarette, his cup sitting on the copper countertop. The uniformed server heard him murmuring a farewell to no one and to everyone.

Outside, the unfolding day afforded the sight of a clutch of students beyond the Chinese butcher shop. Past the corner, they were shuffling around a foam ball in front of the wide open heavy wood door. It was cooler inside the lobby and then beneath the playground roof, and in the shade of the interior courtyard walls. Behind the blue door Valerie was checking her e-mail. Gilles had arrived earlier to make photocopies.

"Hey."

He raised his voice over the copy machine that was disgorging twin triangles.

"Boy it pisses me off to be here, so bad you can't even imagine."

On the T-shirt hanging down to Leopold's knees, two elves were battling.

"I don't feel like starting up again, it's awful."

The first of the students could be heard in the courtyard. Julien, entering, was tan-faced with no glasses marks.

"It's hard coming back."

The copy machine might never stop disgorging.

"No, I mean you cannot even imagine how much it completely pisses me off to be here."

"Oh, there's not that many more days to get through."

I'd had a bad night's sleep.

"Thirty."

Dico hung back from going to the stairway with the rest of them.

"Hurry up."

"Pfffh."

One floor up, Djibril had knocked off Mohammed's springtime cap, and Mohammed had hauled off with a smack that his aggressor evaded by a sidestep into the second floor corridor. When he didn't reappear, I sped up to the landing and looked over to the right. No Djibril. I went along to the fire door at the end, behind which there was still no Djibril. I thought he must have gone up the safety staircase to join us on the third floor.

"That's the price you pay."

The voice coming from a dark corner truss was familiar. The man moved out of the shadow and stopped two yards from me, driving his gaze deep into my brain.

"That's the price you pay. You can't want the number and not want the disorder. You can't want it halfway. Have to just sleep better and keep on wanting."

Again he was missing an arm, the right one.

"We must be modern absolutely."

"Yes."

I was trying to talk over the pneumatic drill.

"What's it called when you say the opposite of what you think and at the same time make it clear that you think the opposite of what you're saying?"

Beneath Indira's enamoured gaze, Abdouolaye twisted his face like he had an ulcer in his brain.

"M'sieur your question, like it gives us a headache."

Mezut's lip was again red from having bled.

"What's the question, m'sieur?"

Mera had changed glasses and come to sit in the front row.

"Isn't that irony?"

"Yes, that's exactly right. When the narrator says that the slaves were treated more humanely by the Europeans than by the African chiefs because they bound them at the ankles instead of at the neck, that's irony. Give me an ironic sentence."

POLO 63 to port side.

"Yes, Bien-Aimé?"

"You're handsome."

"Thank you, but what's the ironic sentence?"

"You're handsome."

"Okay, I see. Thanks."

Mera had changed seats and glasses but not her Kookai pencil case.

"Tomorrow the French teacher will be absent, oh what a pity."

"OK, today's my big day. Yes, Tarek? your turn to put me down."

"This year we did a lot of dictations in French."

From his seat in the front row, Mezut tossed something into the trash basket.

"Mezut, you ask permission to do that."

"It's my red pen, it's leaking."

One of Alyssa's hands held her pencil, chewed down to the lead, the other was pointed to the heavens about to open.

"M'sieur on the television they're oweys sayin about the irony of fate, we don't know what's that mean, y'know?"

"That's kind of special, that one, irony of fate. The irony of fate is when you have the feeling that fate is making fun of humans. For instance, say I'm drowning, and it's my worst enemy who saves my life. See what I mean?"

"It's something like revenge?"

"That's right. I mean, no, not really. Say a soccer player was playing for one club and they drop him and then the next year he's playing for a different team, and in a match against his old club he makes three goals, then the newspapers will say: 'Irony of fate, so-and-so caused the defeat of his old teammates.' Now you see better what I mean?"

"That's what I was saying, it's something like revenge."

"No no, not really. Saying the irony of fate is a little special. And actually the expression is often used wrong."

"Why?"

"For just that reason—it's kind of special."

Marie asked for everyone's attention.

"There's something you should all know."

Everyone turned to listen.

"The mother of Ming—in eighth grade—she's been arrested by Immigration, she might be deported. Her hearing is next week, she could be sent back to China."

Danièle was breathing mist onto a five-centime coin.

"That's crazy, the family's been here for three years already."

"Yes but you know how it is, suddenly one day they decide to round up a batch of illegals, and she got caught in the roundup."

"Not the father?"

"No, not the father. Even though he's in exactly the same situation. Anyhow, you see how it is?"

Everyone did see how it is.

"What I propose is, first that we take up a collection to pay for at least part of the lawyer fees, because they're really high. And then, that we try to get free to go to the trial, see if we can influence things a little."

Under the medieval castle on Leopold's long T-shirt the letters of DEVIL FOREVER dripped blood.

"What about Ming, would he leave too?"

"Nobody knows. In theory, no."

Medieval, with flames leaping up past the battlements.

"It's really horrible because Ming, honestly, he's first class."

Marie set an envelope on the middle table so everyone could slip in a contribution. Everyone did. Geraldine was ruffled.

"Well okay, I was going to announce that I'm pregnant, but I'll wait for another time."

Enthusiastic cries transformed her report into paralipsis.

"I even bought some chocolates."

She untied the ribbon of a gold-cardboard parallelepiped, offered it to those sitting nearest her, and grace fell upon her.

"I have two wishes: that Ming's mom gets to stay, and that my child turns out as intelligent as Ming."

The text was about a miners' strike. As soon as she finished reading at higher volume than the pneumatic drill, Sandra went on.

"M'sieur what's coal used for?"

"It used to be the main fuel."

Triangular plastic earrings. Black.

"What's fuel I dunno what that means?"

"A thing that burns."

She was the only one not asleep. The text was a bore, the questions in the manual were too hard. I flung myself onto the day's date.

"What important thing happened on the tenth of May?"

A few noses lifted their heads, wondering.

"May 10, 1981—mean anything to you?"

Those noses were pools in contemporary history.

"On May 10, 1981 two things happened, and one of them kind of blocked out the other."

Born on January 3, 1989, Aissatou stirred her neurons beneath her black bandana.

"An assassination attempt?"

"At that time there weren't as many of those as there are now. The fashion was more for disco."

1981 had no wake-up effect on anyone. Not even on Sandra, who had vanished and who I realized only later had crossed through the wall.

"Okay, the tenth of May is also my sister's birthday, but nobody really cares about that."

Soumaya uttered a skanky cry.

"How old's your sister, m'sieur?"

"Guess."

All kinds of numbers came thick and fast, running from twelve to fifty-two.

"OK, I'll tell you that some other time. On May 10, 1981, François Mitterrand was elected President of the Republic, and Bob Marley died. Obviously nobody talked about Bob Marley because Mitter-rand's election was a matter of great importance at the time."

"How did Bob Marley die, m'sieur?"

"He died when he saw that Mitterrand had been elected."

"Is that true?"

"Completely true."

Perhaps thrust out by the stench of orange, two sheets of paper fell from my newly opened locker. I picked them up and saw that they were two incident slips from Chantal.

PLACE: ROOM 102

DATE: 10/05

ACCOUNT OF INFRACTION:

Mariama stands up without my authorization to go throw something in the trash can. I indicate that she is not to get up without my authorization. She looks me straight in the eye and retorts: "Oh really! I didn't know. But it's too late now anyhow." This student's insolence requires me to ask for a punishment, as her behavior and her incessant chatter are becoming a real nuisance for the proper conduct of the lesson.

PLACE: ROOM 102

DATE: 10/05

ACCOUNT OF INFRACTION:

I ask Dico to be quiet for the umpteenth time. He mumbles: Okay okay, she really breaks my balls, that lady. This conduct together with endless talking are becoming a noisy nuisance. I ask that Dico apologize and that he be at the least put in detention, as his conduct is becoming unmanageable.

Leaning back on his tufted bench, the Principal gestured to me that he wouldn't be much longer. And in fact, a minute later he rose to bid goodbye to an adult and Vagbema.

"You must understand that this Disciplinary Council was called only after many efforts to bring Vagbema to order, and that, whatever penalty is decided the day after tomorrow, it will have an educational purpose."

The adolescent stared at his laceless sneakers and the adult nearly bumped into me, still blinded by the words of the principal who, leaning back again, pointed me to the armchair his guest had occupied.

"Is this for the second practice exam?"

"You, here's the topic, we just have to make photocopies."

He had tacked the stapled sheets above his ebony-colored wooden desk. He glanced over them.

"Marguerite Duras—that's good. You like Duras?"

"No, but that's all right."

"I've seen the petition about Ming's mother. Let's hope that it will carry a little weight."

Zineb the secretary appeared in the doorway, blue plastic earrings.

"Our dear Mamadou is asking to get his hat back, what do I tell him?"

"Tell him that he has to ask in writing, and sign it."

"He says he needs it right now."

"In that case, tell him it's eighty-five degrees out."

He slipped the exam topics into a folder marked "Canteen."

"And the new student in 9-c—is that working out?"

"Yes. He doesn't do anything but he's quiet."

"You know why he's here?"

"No, actually."

He hesitated like a schoolboy pretending embarrassment before admitting some smart move he's proud of.

"Oh, I can tell you, now."

He took three steps to close the door and sat down beside me, right at my ear. He was chuckling into the collar of his green shirt, black tie.

"Well, he has an unfortunate vice."

His voice had dropped to a murmur.

"The young man has formed the unpleasant habit of masturbating in class."

"Oh?"

"Yes, his particular thing is masturbation."

He chuckled again.

"So his counselor called me yesterday and she had an odd way of telling me about all that. She said we should be careful because he was extremely well developed."

Someone knocked, it was the secretary.

"Mahmadou says the written request would take him too long, and if he doesn't get his hat back right this minute he's going to have real problems."

"I'll be right there."

He waited till the door had closed again.

"That's our main problem, we've got students who are too well-developed."

All the participants notified were present in the study hall, rearranged for the occasion, except for the person of interest. His mother was representing him.

"I've been calling him for a while now, but his telephone is turned off. He did say he's coming, though."

The principal laid out the charges lodged against the student. Eight serious offenses since the start of the year, one per month. He ended by asking for a permanent expulsion. That way Vagbema would have the chance to recast himself somewhere else, and at the same time to put some distance between himself and his twin brother Désiré. There is a place for everyone in the educational system.

The counselor in charge of the case pointed out that the father's blindness gave his sons a sense of impunity, that Vagbema was only doing all this to deal with his distress, that in primary school Vagbema used to turn aside to weep when he was scolded.

A parent rep argued that being in class 7-A was probably disturbing to him. Bastien retorted that Vagbema was a major factor in making 7-A a disturbing class.

The mother ran into her son's answering service three or four times more. She spoke up when it was her turn, said he should be given a chance, that he would do better in eighth grade, that she would be sending him back to their village for the summer, that there were some relatives down there who were teachers and would take him in hand. That was all she had to say, and she was asked to leave the room during the deliberations. Although she closed the door behind her, the principal spoke in low confidential tones.

"I should apprise you of a further detail so that you know all the givens in the situation. I spoke with the father a little yesterday to prepare for this Disciplinary Council meeting and, in fact, it seems the man is convinced that his son is under a spell. Privately, he believes the same to be true about his elder son, who also came through our school, and whose behavior was in fact fiendish."

We voted for permanent expulsion.

Angel with wings unfurled on his long T-shirt, Leopold was rejoicing.

"Overall, there's not a single full week left."

Valerie was checking her e-mails with an ear to the room.

"How do you figure that?"

"Well look, we have this long weekend, the next week there's a strike, the week after that the Monday's a holiday, I mean see, there's always something."

On her screen Valerie had clicked Reply, then typed "Can't wait for the beach" followed by three exclamation points. For Geraldine it was going to be twins. Lina was the last to hear.

"That's great."

"Yes, but you right away wonder what you're gonna wind up with."

Leopold's angel was laughing about something or other, and maybe it was an evil angel, the exterminating type, its goodness just a front, he was come down to earth to cleanse it of the human species suspected of too much goodness, but for the moment, Marie was not worrying about that possibility.

"The lawyer's been paid, that's good anyhow."

"Oh?"

"She says the more of us that turn up at the trial, the greater weight it could have. So I asked to have classes cancelled for the period it's scheduled, the idea being that way we'll get the biggest number of colleagues there."

"And with the students, we doing anything with them?"

"Yeah I thought about that, but the problem is that I'm not sure Ming would like them all to know about it, you see. We should find out from him, really. You have his class today?"

"I've got them right now, I'll ask him."

In the courtyard the kids in T-shirts were crushing the competition. Abdoulaye had settled down after I asked him to.

"M'sieur it's too hot, we gotta have the class outside."

"You want a Coke with that?"

"Oh, you ride us too much m'sieur."

Ming was climbing the stairs ahead of the others. The best thing would have been to ask him to stop there so we could talk. I would have told him It's really terrible what's happening to you, but we're here for you, you know, and we're here because it's terrible, and also because you're admirable, you're a jewel, you're the proof of life, your brain is a masterpiece and so is your soul, would it bother you if we told the kids what's going on so they could do something from their end too about the trial? Ming would have listened to me with his eyes on the ground, the way he does when he's concentrating to understand something, and he would have understood, and he would have told me yes it is a little uncomfortable but there's nothing to lose, so okay yes, thank you.

On the third floor, I unlocked the door and let in most of the flock, who were laughing about something or other. When Ming came by me he said hello. I said how's it going? He said fine, and you? I said fine. Once they were settled in, I asked them to take out their grammar notebooks to go over the functions of the adjective.

As I told you, I have your application files here. These are the forms that you will be filling out and which will be examined by the class council. On them you will put down your own final choices for tenth grade, first year of *lycée*. So then, how to fill them out? All right, roughly speaking you have two forms—we won't bother discussing a third, which is specific and doesn't concern you. Form A is for your wishes about the Vocational *lycée* program, Form B is for the General and Technological program. For Form A, you can list four requests in order of your preference. Thus you would put, for instance, secretarial as the first request, and next to that the high school where you'd like to do that program. Then you go to the second request, for instance sewing trades, and again the same thing—you put down the name of the high school that offers that, along with the address and so on that you'll find in the brochure called 'After Middle School' that you were given in December. And so on down the form. You're allowed to make the same vocational request four times listing four different schools, but we'd advise you to vary your choices so there's a substitute solution in case your first choice is denied. For Form B, the General or Technological program, you do the same—four choices, but this time you don't put down a specific area, because in tenth grade it's a non-specific program. You just write in the two prerequisite courses you'd like to do to prepare for the program you're aiming for. For instance, if you hope to go into industrial technology by grade twelve, then obviously there's no point in taking Latin in tenth; conversely it doesn't make sense to do the MPI computer basics course in tenth if you expect to major in literature later on and so forth. So where you see the two "prerequisite programs," you write the name of the one you want and the details on the *lycée* where you'd like to do them—of course for that you'll have to first check that the *lycée* you list does actually offer them. The difference from Form A is that except for your first choice you have to request a *lycée* that's in your sector. Now, what are the sectors? You've got four in all, which correspond roughly to West, East, North and South. We're in the East sector, that is—keep these in mind—the first, second, third, fourth, tenth, eleventh, twelfth, and twentieth *arrondissements*, and obviously this one; so overall you've got to request a *lycée* that's in your sector, that's the way it works, except for your first choice, there you can choose a school that's outside the sector. And when it comes to knowing which form to fill out, A or B, for that you base your decision on the opinion rendered by the class council. If you've been told OK for the General *lycée* program, you fill out Form B, if you've been told no for the General or yes for the Vocational, you fill out Form A. And if you've been told you have to test for the General you fill out both forms, there you are, it's very simple.

Dico was climbing the stairs to class, behind the others but in front of me. Catching up without glancing at him, I told him to speed up, and he mumbled I don give a shit. After a moment of pseudo-reflection, I stopped in my tracks and turned to him, index finger in front of his nose, and he crossed his eyes to look at it.

"You don't talk to me like that."

"What? I just don't care."

He was blocked, trying to go up. I held him back by the arm and he raised his voice.

"You don't touch me like that."

"I won't touch you if you stop."

"You plain don't touch me like that, that's all."

"I won't touch you if you stop, and first off you don't give me orders."

He was near to exploding, my legs quaked.

"Okay take your hands off."

"What's up with you, are you nuts? The other day you were saying I was in a rage against you, but now it looks like you're the one."

He stepped up one stair to defy me.

"All right then, you come with me to the principal."

The class had come down to the landing and were crowded together a few steps above us. Djibril stepped out from the bunch and intervened, pushing his pal back and arguing with him like in a million and a half movies.

"Djibril that's enough, you playing lawman here. We don't need that. And the rest of you go back upstairs, this is no theater here. You, you follow me."

Cut the brain away from the rest, from the quaking legs and the rest. Astoundingly, Dico followed me, though a few yards behind.

"Quit walking like that, why you going to the principal, why you don't stay here? Little fag."

I stopped short in the middle of the courtyard, our voices stepped all over each other.

"What'd you just say, then?"

"Why you don't stay here?"

"Because I want to be rid of you, that's why, simple as that."

"Stay here if you're a man."

"Why? What d'you want us to do exactly, you and me? You wait right there, don't you move."

Walk on with a firm step, don't look up toward the windows where the class was getting a kick out of the scene. The office door was open and I could see a half-dozen students listening to a sermon from the principal. I came back to Dico, who was now sitting on a bench. My voice was low as I leaned in toward him, nose to nose, brain cut away from the rest.

"The principal is busy so you'll wait right there. And obviously I don't want to lay eyes on you again. Tomorrow is a holiday and after that it's the exam, so the question doesn't come up, but Wednesday I don't want to see you in my class."

Mariama had come down to see, and my rage fell onto her.

"What's madame the concierge butting in for?"

"I'm not a concierge, okay."

"Get back upstairs and leave me the hell alone."

Shadow-eyed all over, Gilles set his practice exam papers on the oval table piled up with the others. I started counting them.

"All done? How was it?"

"Yeah, not so hot. Us math types, we're not used to doing dictations, y'know."

"But weren't there actually instructions on the desk? Read the thing aloud all the way through once, then each segment twice, then one more time before we collect the papers."

I began the count again. Tanned all over, Julien put down the final pack of papers. His gaze came to rest on Gilles.

"You don't look so hot."

"Yeah, and on top of it they make me do dictation."

"I just did what the instructions said."

"Yeah but still. The next time I'll ask the French teachers to write the math exam, see how they do."

I went back to counting. Marie mustered the troops.

"For the trial tomorrow, make specially sure that you put it down in the home report booklets that you're going to be absent."

His head blocking out the praying peasant's, Claude questioned Julien.

"You got your transfer, I hear?"

"Yep. To Royan."

"That's so great!"

Valerie was having trouble changing the ink in the copy machine.

"Isn't Royan a city that has ramparts?"

"Yes it is."

"That's really beautiful."

"Yes but we'll be living outside the walls. Full ocean view, we're gonna have a ball. That would do you good, Gilles."

"Besides, you know, I lisp a little, so you should see the students, they don't mind making a big deal of it when you dictate."

I went back to counting.

"Yeah, I dunno. At one point there's a passage about a fur coat in the dictation. Okay, well, I say *peliche* for *pelisse*, see, and since the students don't know what the thing is anyhow they keep asking me to repeat the word, and each time it gets worse."

"Sixty-three. Damn, one short."

"Maybe you made a mistake counting."

"I'll do it again."

Finally, your Honor, I wish to offer the present document to the court's attention. This is a statement prepared by the teachers at the middle school where Madame Shu's son Ming is enrolled in perfectly normal conditions. The whole pedagogic team, of which a large number are here today, asked to testify that Ming has made absolutely remarkable progress in these three years, and that his return to China would be a terrible halt to an exemplary process of assimilation. At the risk of straying into considerations which have no place within these walls, I add that such unanimity among his instructors ultimately persuaded me to take up the defense of a case which *a priori* I, like yourselves, would have considered indefensible. I thank you.

"So it's about this girl—well, actually it's her diary, but she's kind of like all of us, y'know, same as us, super-regular, like she goes to school, it's boring, her parents murder her when she gets a crummy grade, I mean like us all, y'know, and that's why it's so scary you think omigod that could happen to us, y'know."

Sandra, plugged into three different electric plants, had asked to do a book report for the class. I'd said fine, *Go Ask Alice*, all right, yes I've read it, it's very good. We changed places, she at the board, I at the back of the room. From time to time her lifted arms exposed a navel that was the eye of her little potbelly.

"One day she goes to a party, and it's her first time so like she isn't too sure how to act, y'know, but after a while she gets into it, she's dancing and all and at some point she drinks a Coke but there's like some speed in the glass and she didn't know it, y'know, so then she starts freaking out, it's like wow, she's seeing things that aren't there and all, I swear on my mother's life really it is told sooo well, y'know, but okay the problem is that all of a sudden she really gets into that whole thing she like starts taking everything, y'know, shit, heroin, everything, she totally goes off the rails and it's rilly creepy because I tell you this is a girl that's just completely regular, y'know, like us and at the end, well there I didn't exactly understand, at the end they say that she died a week after she wrote the last page of this. Does that mean it's a true story, m'sieur?"

"Not necessarily. Even when they say that this manuscript was found in some old box or whatever, it could still be made up. With this book, I don't know. But the important thing is that all of it could happen, as you said."

A recollection brightened Imani's face.

"Oh, yes, that means it's incredible!"

"No, the opposite: credible, believable. Maybe it's invented, but it's believable, it's like the truth."

"It's the incorrect things you absolutely have to get rid of for the real *Brevet* exam three weeks from now, and that's very simple because you just have to keep them in mind, you see? For instance, remember that in writing, the adverb '*trop*' means 'too much,' not 'very'—that may seem crazy, but in fact the adverb 'too' means exactly what it means to say—it's more a negative idea. When I say, in writing, that 'that man is too generous,' it means that his generosity is excessive—too much—and that in some way or other it could be bad for him. But in speech, at least the way your generation uses it, 'too handsome' means 'very' handsome, and it's positive, only positive. 'He's too handsome' means he is extremely handsome and I adore him—you see? Also, remember that '*en train de*' is written as three words, not two. Almost everyone attached '*en*' to '*train*'—*entrain de*. That's a detail, but it's easy to correct. Same thing for '*eh bien*' with an H; everyone here writes '*et bien*' with a T, yes, yes I assure you, you make that mistake every time, and you're not the only ones. Okay, I'm going back a little to this business of what's oral or spoken language—I remind you that just because you're asked to write a dialogue doesn't mean you're supposed to write the way you speak, you see? In fact, you can never write exactly the way you speak, it's impossible, the best you can do is give the feeling of oral style, of speaking style, that's all. So we avoid starting sentences with 'honestly,' we avoid saying '*on*' for 'we', we avoid using 'serious' as an adverb, the way you kids do all the time when you're talking. That's how it is, there are things that must stay only in oral style—for instance there, I just said '*y'a des choses*,' and in speech people always say '*y'a*' rather than '*il y a*,' but in writing, even when it's dialogue, you have to write '*il y a*,' that's the way it is, it just takes a little thought, and if you don't think about it, well, I can't exactly say it means points deducted but it doesn't help you, and look you see I just said '*si vous pensez pas*' and '*ca vous aide pas*,'—it doesn't help you—both times I left out the *ne* that's needed to complete the negative meaning. Why did I? Because I'm speaking, this is oral form, and in the oral form it's rare for us to put in the '*ne*' for negation, except when we're purposely adopting a formal, elevated language, you see? But in writing, you do put it in. So on the exam, in every single case you must put in the *ne,* you check every negative and insert *ne* or *n* apostrophe before the verb and the *pas.* Always do it, even if in your own mind you think it doesn't matter."

The population around the U was fanning itself with a flapping file folder or a notepad. Through the wide-open windows, a bird astonishingly whistled the *Internationale.* At the head of the U, the principal was initialing forms and piling them at a corner of his table.

"Djibril is next."

"Omigod, that one."

"What, he's still acting up since last term?"

"No, but the gaps in his learning—it's wild."

"Yes, so many gaps."

"You wonder how he even got as far as eighth grade."

The principal detests that kind of remark. Doesn't let it show. Jokes.

"Well, I suppose he went from kindergarten to first grade then from first grade to second then from second to third, and so on."

Jacqueline does not joke.

"Yes but really now it's gotten impossible, we have to find him something else. Would a vocational ninth grade be worth a try?"

This was addressed to the psychologist guidance counselor.

"Yes, I've talked to him about it. The problem is that he has no idea what he could do in the vocation area. It doesn't connect with his interests at all. I don't think he's one of those students who needs to lay his hands on something more tangible. On the contrary, he's very abstract. His aptitude tests come up with some very odd results—they swing between puzzling and brilliant."

From childhood on, Luc had never missed a chance to kid around.

"Could be he's some kind of supertalent and nobody realized it."

A wave of snickers ran around the U, stopped short at the chair of the principal, whose body was not conductive for that energy.

"If he has no plan we can't send him into a 'ninth grade with vocational option.'"

"Well then, in that case, he repeats eighth grade."

"You think that would change anything?"

For Gilles, nothing would change anything.

"A regular ninth is really not possible."

As if decided by a snap of the fingers, a violent draft pushed the door against its frame and sent Djibril's file flying; lifted a yard above our heads, it made a loop or two, then began a slow descent like a glider to exactly the spot it had taken off from, between the principal's naked tanned forearms.

Everyone was listening to Valerie.

"Down there, salaries are better than here by 1.53 percent."

Coiled around a staff, the serpent on Leopold's T-shirt was

trying to hypnotize Rachel. Geraldine's breasts were growing in proportion to her twins. Lina took a seat in the ragged circle.

"Where's that?"

"In La Réunion—I got my assignment yesterday."

"Oh wow, luck!"

"Really. Down there taxes are 30 percent lower."

Claude took a seat in the ragged circle.

"Where's that?"

"In La Réunion, I got my assignment yesterday."

"Oh wow, bingo!"

"Really. The TVA is lower too. But you have to consider gasoline is very high down there."

Bastien took a seat in the ragged circle.

"Where's that?"

"In La Réunion, I got my assignment yesterday."

"Oh wow, cool."

Discouraged by Rachel's eyeglasses, Leopold's serpent turned its powers onto Gilles, telling him,

"Trust."

"Trust what? You make me laugh."

"Trust me, that's enough."

"I don't trust anyone."

Marie joined the ragged circle.

"Well, the verdict is in—we lost."

"Oh?"

"Could've predicted it, in this kind of case only one out of a hundred gets off. But the lawyer believed in it."

Everyone had turned away from the neo-Réunionian citizen.

"It's final?"

"There's an appeal. That'll gain a little time, but still."

"And Ming—what's he going to do?"

"He'll wait, like everyone else."

Pleased with his ploy, the principal had snatched me into his office, looking like a conspirator.

"I managed to fix it so the teachers who mark the exams here will only be marking the students from just this one school."

"Oh?"

Pleased with his ploy.

"That way, you understand, they won't be making comparisons with the papers from some school that's—shall we say, better favored; they'll see only the papers from here, which could allow higher scores, you get the idea?"

"Smart move."

"Yes, I must say I'm rather pleased with my ploy. Have a coffee?"

Three steps to the machine and then his necktie hung above the cups.

"No because otherwise, you understand, the good papers from here, set next to good papers from other places, well of course it's stupid but they look just average. You take your coffee strong?"

"Yes."

"All right, sure, it's not going to change the face of the world as much as my grandma's nose, but you never know, it could raise the percentage a bit."

Mohammed the monitor appeared in the doorway, alongside a T-shirt with a leaping puma.

"Can I leave this person with you?"

"And to what do we owe the honor of his visit?"

"Yesterday he told us three students beat him up, and today when we ask him for their names he says he bumped into a wall."

"Fine thank you, sit down Sheik Omar. So just like that, you bumped into a wall all by yourself?"

The so-named sat down, a glaring welt in the middle of his forehead. His eyes followed the principal's little coffee spoon.

"Yes."

"It's true this place is awfully small, so naturally if a person doesn't watch out he can hit the wall."

Monitor Mohammed, again.

"That little girl in sixth grade with the asthma attack—do we let her go home?"

The decider decided yes, and called me to witness by lowering his voice.

"That asthma attack—it's a little pollen allergy, but let it go."

His spoon had ceased its stirring, and Sheik Omar's pupils no longer moved.

They had just copied down the essay topics and were doodling while they figured out what to say.

—Describe your first encounter with some friend, keeping within your own viewpoint.
—Will Chirac be able to deal with the consequences of this second electoral setback in three months, or will he decide to hide behind yet another massive abstention in the European vote?

More than ever, questions arose, and of course Jiajia raised her hand. "M'sieur, he hitting me back there."

Back there was Dico.

"Pfffh oweys talkin bullshit that one."

"Well you know, it's funny—I kind of tend to believe her, I don't know why. Dico hitting somebody—a person is a little tempted to believe it."

"Talkin bullshit I never touch her I don give a shit about her."

"If that's the case then you just go not give a shit outside."

He stood up, pushing back his chair with a rough shove of the thigh. I pretended to dive back into Metro. He dawdled meticulously over putting his things together. Starting his trek toward the door, he flung a pen at the back of Jiajia's neck. I met him at the landing.

"Follow me to the principal's office."

Very swiftly, I outpaced him as he dragged along behind. I crouched to retie my shoelace so that he would catch up and pass me. He caught up and passed me.

"Talks bullshit talk this guy, he tyin his lace little fag."

I caught up to him in the courtyard. He stood still.

"Why we goin to the office?"

"You think you can hit somebody like that and nothing would happen?"

He started shouting.

"Bullshit talk I din hit her jus bullshit talk her sayin that."

"Throwing a pen, what do you call that?"

"That's not hittin, hittin I'll show you what hittin is."

"Oh yeah you're gonna show me?"

"Yeah I'll show you."

I resumed my march toward the office and he followed me, the jerk.

"You know you can keep saying *tu* to me all you want, I completely do not give a damn, you wouldn't believe how much I don't give a damn."

"Okay yeah I'll *tutoie* you, if I feel like it I'll *tutoie* you."

Again we were motionless, now in front of the office door.

"And I tell you I don't give a damn if you *tutoie* me."

"An I don't give a damn if I *tutoie* you, why we goin in there anyhow?"

"And you, why are you still coming to school? It's the end of the year now. Nobody would be bothering you about attendance, why are you still coming in here to drive us crazy?"

"That's why."

"You know why you keep coming in? You keep coming because you don't know what else to do. Because otherwise you'd go nuts."

"That's enough quit talkina me."

"And you know why you'd go nuts? Because your life is just nothing. Because you've got a lousy life."

"Is yours any better?"

"Yeah, mine is a thousand times better than yours, coming into school because you've got nothing else to do. At least I'm not spending my life in a place I can't stand."

"Get out that's all quit talkina me."

"And you know why you keep coming here? Because you're not strong. You're not strong enough to stay away."

"And you're a fighter?"

"Yeah, I'm a fighter."

"Ohh yeah, that's right you're a fighter."

"Right."

I opened the door. The principal was standing right there, taking care of a kid with a nosebleed.

"I bring you today's Dico."

In the guise of urging him forward, I slipped my arm behind his back, and my hand touched him lightly. He exploded, started screaming, writhing, a horse caught in his stall with a storm coming on. Until that moment casual, the principal now stepped in.

"Calm down, Dico."

I overplayed the relaxed procedural tone.

"Dico hit a girl in the class, so I thought it was a good idea to bring him along to you."

He shouted louder yet.

"I din hit her, why's he saying that, quit saying I hit her I'm sick of this let me alone now that's it I'm outa here."

Dico kicked a chair, and its back danced across the room and hit the desk of the frightened secretary. He headed toward the door, broke through my pseudo-resistance without his full force, so he did not really do a thing I was not really stopping him from doing. And it was beside the point for the principal to say,

"Let him go, it's better."

He rushed toward the interior courtyard rather than toward the outside. While I was picking up the chair and telling the gaping secretary It's all right, the principal caught up with the other jerk and blocked his way into the courtyard, pointing to the exit door through the play yard.

"No no no, you don't go this way, you go through there."

I moved closer to avoid the look of a person keeping his distance. The principal's finger still pointed to the heavy wooden door.

"If you want to leave, you leave for good, and that's that. As far as we're concerned, we don't want to see you again."

He crossed the covered yard, stepped into the lobby, and disappeared past the solid wood door.

It was first day in February, 2001, I was in class of mathematic, my grand mother she have announced to me that I was going study in France. She said you are big boy Ming. I was very glad but sometime I was sad because I have to leave my grand parents and my friendes. After a long time in plane, I was arriving in France. It is a country libertine and humanity. Six months I was register in the Valmy school, it is a very clean school. I was in a new people class and it was not just me alone there, there were other Chinese students that I did not know them. My seat was at the side of Jacky, this was a very nice person and who liked to talked. During some days of exchanges, we became friends. He is Pakestan, that is a country that is next to China. He was in France two years more than me and he talked much better than me French. It was one year we were in the same class, and in second year I changed school, it was here, the Mozart middle school. But we still have always communicate on the telephone.

It was too calm. No movement distracted from the scene. The walls were drawing together and would crush us all.

"Hakim you must know this—when exactly is the opening game?"

He lifted his nose out of his paper, interrupted in his count of the scenes in Act II.

"It's Saturday. At five o'clock. Portugal-Greece."

Aissatou, black bandanna with a whole planetarium underneath it, "M'sieur, who you for?"

I walked down into the aisle and answered only when I was leaning against the closet at the back.

"I'm for Spain."

Would Faiza get the life she dreamed of?

"You not even for France?"

"Well no, not really."

Hinda resembled somebody or other and letters spelling INACCESSIBLE striped across her chest.

"On the life of my grandmother back in the bled, they're too handsome the players on the French team."

Soumaya cried out as if someone had snatched off her cellphone pendant.

"You are crazy in the head, they're just too ugly!"

Zidane really looked like a macaque-head with that hair. But nobody cares how he looks, the important thing is he plays real good and that's all, and even if he would be all green all over it's the same thing you shouden be sayin nothin about how he looks, if he's a martian or if he stinks from shit or anything. Yeah but still they're too handsome. England they're more handsome that's why me I'm for them. That one there she makes me laugh those guys all so ugly with they old heads, they look like they got messed up in they momma's belly. Beckham was he messed up in his momma's belly? If Beckham got messed up then you, it's a waste a time you even got born. Henry he's too handsome. You kiddin his head it isn't even straight, looks crazy like he come out butt end first. How his head looks I don't give a shit pardon m'sieur.

No problem.

The bellies on Geraldine and Sylvie were now equally large, the former having caught up with the latter because it was twins. If they were boys, she would be naming them Leo, Lucas, Clement. If it was girls, Lea, Marguerite, Manon. Chantal wasn't pregnant, and she charged into the room in a fury, her breasts ahead of the rest of her.

"It's intolerable to stand for that. These two kids walk into my classroom and call me a dirty whore, very pleasant, I swear."

Jean-Philippe shook his head in misery.

"Some of them, we've got to tell them straight out just not to come in anymore except for counseling. Like during Ramadan, it would be better if they just stayed home."

Geraldine thought that it was probably harder to keep the fast staying home, saying,

"It's the 7-AS who should be forbidden to come in."

Leopold would have signed onto that with both hands.

"You can't do a thing with them, that's how it is."

"No listen, there's no reason to blame anyone. Like my mother used to say, You don't make stallions out of workhorses."

"Me, next year I'm not taking any eighth grade, you can believe me on that."

Sylvie turned to me with a mischievous little look I detested.

"You, you always have eighth grades, you'll get to discover the whole lot. We'll see what you're made of."

"Yeah, right, we'll see what I'm made of. I'll take two classes, even—two eighth grades—so I can be sure to get a maximum of pissers. First I'll calm the pissers down and then I'll make them into students who're comfortable with grammar and inventive at writing. I'll take workhorses and make them into stallions, that's my specialty. I'm a teaching genius, I am. I invented the pedagogue's stone, okay?"

In the courtyard a swarm of ninth-grade girls buzzed around Rachel.

"That's really not right, mam."

"Really mam that's not right."

"Mam that's really not right."

With a look Rachel told me I don't know what to do, this morning I suggested every student should leave some mark behind in the school, here on this wall. The problem is, half of them painted the characters from their countries of origin, and the next period I had to ask the sixth-graders to cover them up, and look now, it's World War III.

"Really mam that's going too far."

"It's going too far really mam."

"Mam that's really going too far."

On the wall, twenty handprints in all colors crowded over one another. Here and there were names, designs, coded word-forms, and yes, a few scribbles meant to cover something over, which Rachel was trying to justify.

"National names in a secular institution—it's just not allowed, that's all."

Off to one side, Soumaya was fulminating.

"That's it. Rilly all you want us to do is write France or nothing. But me if I feel like putting Tunisia I'm putting Tunisia, you want everybody should be like you that's no good, hear."

Salimata was arguing further as she tore leaves off a lowhanging branch.

"Honest mam that's not right to ask the sixth grade kids to come cross out Mali and Senegal and all, it's like you're crossing out students that come from there it's not right."

Rachel's feet were tiny in her erotic pink thong sandals.

"I told you at the beginning, I said no countries."

Katia was wearing pink shoes too, but they were Converses with ALL STAR written in a circle on the ankle.

"M'sieur you agree with us like it's not right to cross students out?"

"I don't know if it's right, but couldn't you find anything more original to write than names of countries? If it was me in the circumstances, if somebody asked me to make up some sign to represent myself, I wouldn't have put France or Vendée, you know?"

ALL STAR.

"What's that mean, surcummstan, m'sieur?"

"It's a country. There are people who live in Surcummstan."

"You're always kidding around m'sieur, that's not right."

"'In this circumstance' means in this case, in this situation, here and now, within these walls—in these circumstances, on that wall there."

From the start, Aissatou was listening without joining in. Directly under the full sun, her ears cocked, she concentrated on all the terms of the debate. My whole life I will remember Aissatou.

"So what you woulda put m'sieur?

"I don't know. The name of some singer I like. Or somebody in sports. Or a writer. I would've put Rimbaud, that's it."

"Who's that?"

"A guy your age."

Over near the restrooms, Soumaya was a boxer being held back from fighting.

"That teacher she says free expression but we can't even put down what we want, that's not free expression, that stinks that's all."

Rachel was paralyzed with impotence. However, Salimata had swallowed her own resentment a little by now.

"M'sieur, what's that thing you said before?"

"What thing?"

"I dunno, you said France and then some other thing I dunno what."

"I must have said France and the Vendée."

"That's it. What is that, that vonday?"

"It's a *département*, a region of France. That's where I was born. What I meant was I kind of don't care about it all that much, see?"

"Is it far away?"

"You see this wall? Well it's past that. Way way past that."

Katia spoke up:

"Isn't it kind of like where the peasants live, m'sieur?"

"Yes, sort of."

For the last individual help session, I asked them to list twenty things they'd learned over the year in eighth grade. Twenty things that they didn't know before and knew now. They set to work without fuss. Walking through the rows, craning over shoulders, I realized that they were only partly fulfilling the assignment.

"Don't stop with just telling me you learned Pythagoras's theorem. I want you to write it out, too. Sofiane, I saw that you wrote the term '*sans-culottes*' and nothing more. That won't do at all, you've got to tell me who those people were. Especially when two lines farther on you list 'the French Revolution' as a separate item. Maybe there's some connection."

Reading Mody's sheet when he turned it in half an hour later, I was forced to observe that he hadn't adjusted his shot. It was a string of chapter titles, all kinds of topics jumbled together, but without specifics on the knowledge they implied. All the papers were like that, except for Katia's.

"I learned Pythagoras's theorem: in the triangle ABC right angle at B, there is: CA (squared) = AB (squared) + CB (squared). I learned about absolute rule, the reign of Louis XIV, the trade triangle: commerce among European merchants, with black slaves traded for products that were rare in Europe. In French I learned the passive and the active voices, example: the dog bit the girl, the girl was bitten by the dog. I learned how to say '*il y a*' in English: 'ago.' I learned some chemical terms: Oxygen = O, Nitrogen = N, Iron = Fe. I learned some Spanish vocabulary: *collège* = *colegio, il y a* = *hay, vivre* = *vivir, cachette* = *escondite*, and also conjugation in Spanish, e.g. the endings in the present tense: *e-as-a-amos-ais-an*. I learned the English irregular verbs: sing sang sung = *chanter*; drive drove driven = *conduire*; meet met met = *rencontrer*; be was been = *être*; do did done = *faire*. Also the present perfect in English, e.g.: she has just driven the water = *elle vient juste de boire de l'eau*. I learned that in physics you always have to put a voltmeter in an electric shunt. I learned about cubist art: drawing that has several viewpoints."

Ming finished after everyone else and only turned in his paper when the ninth-graders, with Gibran and Arthur in front giggling over something, started into the room for the next period. I would read it the next day.

"**Eighth grade** is a most important year in the middle schools, so a person must work harder and I learned many thing in eighth grade.

French is the most difficult material for me, but I have worked hard so I have learned things in french class. I capable to understand small books, I have learned some vocabularies that I was not knowing before. Because of french class I believe I have augmented my ability in the writings. The mathe is a not a very hard subject for me. In mathe I learned what is the Pythagoras: in the triangle ABC where B is a right angle, there is: CA (squared) = AB (squared) + CB (squared). History is a hard subject for me also, but I have learned things also, I know what is the triangular commerce. It is a commerce between Europe, Africa, and America, they exchange cloth and slaves. I know what is the new machines of communications in the 19th century, it is the electric telegraph and cable under water. In English I have learn many things too. I know what is the present perfective. It is HAVE (in the present) + the past participle. I also know how to make the future, it is S + will + V + Comp. And I learn many other thing."

The world is only a bottomless sewer where formless creatures creep and writhe upon mountains of muck.

"Well? What's the figure of speech in this passage?"

Mezut looked as though he hadn't slept for a hundred years.

"A main clause."

"Yes, there *is* a main clause in the sentence, quite right, but that's not what I'm asking for."

Alyssa will have taken everything in.

"It's a metaphor."

"Yes. And we'd say an extended metaphor, because it stretches over a whole lexical field—this one could be called a lexical field of decay."

Under unceasing dental assault, Alyssa's pencil had wound up twisted into a question mark.

"But m'sieur that's not true what they're saying there."

"What *he's* saying, not what *they* are saying. Perdican is speaking alone. What's not true?"

"How the world is rotten and all."

"Ah but that's not the only thing he's saying, actually. Look at the last sentence: 'It is I who have lived and not some factitious being created by my pride and my ennui.'"

"Factitious, I don't know what that is."

"Factitious means false, artificial, fraudulent. But to really understand the reversal from one sentence to the next, we have to reread the whole tirade right through. We'll do that next time, now I'd like to finish looking for metaphors."

Alyssa was already devouring the tirade with her silent lips moving. Djibril hadn't glanced at the thing once throughout the period, nor opened his mouth until now, without warning, like a punctual time bomb.

"'Nyhow this a school fulla corpses."

"I don't see the connection, Djibril."

Cellphone on a pendant.

"Just issa school fulla corpses."

"If it's a school full of corpses, why do you keep on coming in, when you know that this late in the school year nobody's going to ask you for explanations?"

A MALIAN SOCCER FEDERATION badge was sewn to the right breast of his satin pullover.

"All a bunch a corpses, no arguing about it, that's all."

"I'm not arguing, I'm saying why do you keep coming in to a school full of corpses when nobody's making you?"

"I'll do what I want. That's all."

"But it's *not* what you want, that's what I'm saying. You can't want to come in to a school full of corpses."

"How you know what I want? You just talking that's all."

He stood up. Pulled his summertime cap down to his eyebrows. Opened the door with no roughness. Closed it without slamming and that's all.

I was supposed to stay available in a room on the third floor. I hoped that no student would come in for review. *It's something unpredictable but in the end it's right, I hope you had the time of your life.* At eleven o'clock the sound of footsteps grew louder in the stairway. Four feet. Two pairs. Katia and Sandra.

"Hello, m'sieur."

"You want to work?"

"Yes m'sieur."

"Sit down, I'll give you an exercise."

They sat down, I gave them an exercise on the conditional, which they ended up not doing. They had come to talk, Katia excited like a flea in CONVERSE ALL STARS and Sandra plugged in to a dozen power grids.

"M'sieur are we gonna pass the exam?"

"No."

"M'sieur you shouldn't kid about that, will we pass it or not?"

"Look if you work a little you've got a chance. That's why it's good that you came in."

Darting in breathless came Hakim, Imani, Mohammed Ali, Haj, Habiba, Aissatou. And Hinda. They sat down without opening their bags.

"M'sieur can we have a debate?"

"What about the exam, nobody cares?"

"Debates is better."

"Yes, but there's no debate in the exam."

They began talking about same-sex marriage, the girls weren't against it, the boys totally, with Hakim making a disgusted face as he gave his opinion. Aissatou was considering, Mohammed Ali said that's not the way to make love, Sandra said that in the bled girls would let themselves be sodomized so they would still be virgins when they married, you know? It's crazy, the guys go like oh, they don't want no vulgar girls, when them they're animals themselves, you know. The girls sometimes they even go get sewed up again, Katia added, just even kissing in public you can't do that in Morocco, said Hinda-looking-like-somebody-I-don't-know-who, and then Sandra gave her a sly, allusive look.

"Not like in France, huh Hinda?"

Hinda pretended not to understand so as to keep alive a teasing that brought her only pleasure. Sandra persisted, rolling her eyes like a pastry eater.

"M'sieur Hinda's in love."

"Ah?"

Picking up speed as she went on like a turbine, Sandra was unstoppable.

"M'sieur don't you think she's beautiful, Hinda?"

"She is very pretty."

Katia gave a my oh, my! and took up the cry.

"Don't you think she looks like Jenifer in *Star Ac*, y'know, on TV? Everybody says so, I think it's too true she really does look like her."

The bell made them converge mechanically toward the door while continuing to discuss the matter and wishing me happy vacation between sentences.

"You too. But you've still got a week of review to do, don't forget."

I was hoping Aissatou, Sandra and Hinda would say a special goodbye, but no.

"Some reunion, it was really worth it bringing us all back for this. Okay I'm outa here."

Jean-Philippe was not happy. His unmarked backpack disappeared through the blue door. On Leopold's T-shirt an unappealing eagle glided above the letters of RHAPSODY.

"You had a lot of people come in yesterday for the review sessions?"

Marie had just discovered the front/back function on the photocopier.

"Yes, maybe twenty or so out of my two ninth grades."

"Dico there?"

"No. I don't think we're going to see any more of him."

Elise had gotten fat.

"If he wants to pass he'd better get a lot less lousy in physics."

Having set his gaze on Elise to listen to her, Claude went on. "Did you get yourself a good rest over these two months?"

"Don't ask. I slept, ate, ate, slept. A dream. I got fat, in fact."

The unappealing eagle would soon land on the letter H.

"You're not done yet, either, what with tomorrow's meal."

Claude looked at Elise's waistline.

"You *are* coming, aren't you?"

Forty-five kilos, Elise had put on.

"Yes, yes, sure I'm coming. The teachers, fine. It's the students, I'll need a little time before I'm ready to see them again."

The H in RHAPSODY had only a few minutes to live.

"And that reception at the mayor's office—is everybody going?"

Geraldine didn't want to know whether her twins were boys, girls, or a mix of the two. The painted peasants behind her were praying upright for the former. That would make for more man-power.

"What exactly is this reception?"

From now on it would be written RAPSODY.

"It's some soccer tournament, I think."

I'd had a bad night's sleep.

"No, the soccer is the day after."

The peasants prayed and prayed, the fields were dry, that was all they could do. Marie mechanically took the scissors out of my hands.

"Do we have to go? Because for me, soccer, thanks but no thanks."

Inexplicably, the copy machine began to work on its own, spitting out white sheets much more slowly than usual, one every ten seconds, but it seemed as though that might go on indefinitely, the same useless virginal paper cloned into infinity, and Leopold made a move to fix it then gave up the idea of breaking into the repetition, so he could only talk along with it.

"I didn't work Wednesdays last year, I'm not going to start now."

He wouldn't be going either to the reception or to the tournament. I would be.

The principal, in his good gray special-events jacket, was not sweating.

"I worry there won't be enough chairs."

In fact there were fewer than three hundred, filling a rectangle that owed its contours to the four walls of the great hall with its polished wood floor on which jostled six hundred sneakers, American, English, and German brands. At the back, a stage filled the breadth of the hall and waited for the principal, perched upon it directly beneath the chandelier dripping with crystals, to achieve silence. All he achieved was spates of static from the microphone.

"Many times over the course of this year I have told you to be quiet. I often told you things like 'Be quiet' or 'Calm down.' And today I must do so again. But I would also like to tell you other sorts of things. For instance that you have talent, which you've often shown us. That everyone here can succeed if only you want to. For a person only learns if he wants to learn, if he commits to a project. And because he believes in you as well, His Honor the mayor of the 19th *arrondissement* was eager to welcome you here."

Claude was sweating as he monitored, on the little digital rectangle, the life his camera lens embraced: the principal stepping down from the stage against a mural of the Republic, with Abdelkrimo and Fatih figures in the background, Ming camped square in the shot (nothing would get him out of there), Frida glowing, Mezut somber, Sandra crossing the shot at a run, Khoumba perfect to the end in her stance of ignoring me, and a foreground of students fanning themselves with sheets of paper drawn from the backpacks they'd laid on their knees to applaud Zaina and Hélène, who, holding mikes loosely, had taken up positions beneath the enormous chandelier to act out their introductory sketch.

"Well gee, Zaina, that's some look you've got on your face, what's wrong?"

"I can't dance, I can't sing, I can't act, I don't know what I can do."

"Just watch the other kids, you'll see, you'll like it."

At that signal, Alyssa stepped to the front of the stage. Thus elevated, she stood four yards tall, like a question mark grown large by eating all the questions it had ever punctuated. Her voice did not tremble.

"Adieu, Camille. Go back to your convent, and when they tell you those dreadful tales that have poisoned your mind, answer them what I tell you now: All men are liars, inconstant, false, chatterers, hypocrites, prideful and cowardly, contemptuous and sensual; all woman are faithless, artful, vain, inquisitive, and depraved. The world is nothing but a bottomless sewer, where formless creatures creep and writhe on mountains of muck. But in this world there is one thing holy and sublime: that is the union of two of these imperfect, frightful beings. We are often deceived in love, often hurt, often unhappy. But we love. And when we stand at the rim of the grave, we turn to look back, and we say, 'I have often suffered, sometimes erred, but I have loved. It is I who have lived, not some factitious being created by my pride and my ennui.'"

She withdrew without bowing, and was replaced by two nameless girls beneath the chandelier hanging weary with its weight. To a dancehall tune they began moving symmetrically around a chair like magician's assistants in sparkling costume, then disappeared amid applause they had not expected. Hélène and Zaína reappeared, the latter taking up the sketch again.

"You call that dancing? No, really, it's nonsense, that's not dancing."

"You think they can do better?"

"You're kidding."

"You really think they could better?"

"Go on, of course they can do better."

"I think you're right."

A boombox began to play, and set atremble the heavy darkened chandelier beneath which, nearly touching it with their arms stretched to the stars, the same two nameless girls reappeared. They had swiftly switched their tapestry-flowered skirts for black tights and close fitting red T-shirts. In perfect synchrony, they alternated undulations and stiffenings of their limbs, arabesques and shudders of the neck, imperiously urged on by the muted beat and shrill chanting of the English-language singer. Their feet leapt on the planks, the great slack chandelier trembled.

Hakim, Michael and Amar stomped angrily back from the soccer field.

"This school sucks, m'sieur."

I stopped.

"What do you mean, the school sucks?"

Hakim was wearing the Algeria team shirt, Michael the one for Paris-St.Germain, and their voices tangled together.

"We won all our matches and then that bastid principal he disqualifies us, thass not right m'sieur."

"He never even told us, I swear m'sieur it's true on the Koran and Mecca it's true. They never tell us it's only one class on a team, an we took some 9-bs in with us, and the bastid he just disqualifies us, I mean no way!"

"Me I'm like, fine I'm going home, the bastid goes like Thass right go on home, I mean m'sieur it's a ripoff, man."

"Well yeah but if you guys didn't follow the rules, what do you want the principal to do? Where's the field, anyhow?"

"Way in the back, behind the gray building."

Behind the gray building, way in the back, was the field. A handful of my colleagues and the principal had settled behind a goal, around and on a stone bench. I nodded toward the field where a team of adults faced a bunch of students.

"Who is that playing against us?"

"It's the 8-as. They're really good."

Just then, Nassuif took off from the middle of the field, raised his head then passed to Baidi, who just stretched out his leg for a flick over Serge the dean, who was playing goalie. The ball bounced slowly back into the net. Ali came over and high-fived the striker and they trotted back to their end, two backs in tandem beneath the great friendly clouds. Danièle broke faith.

"Right now we're ahead by one goal but it won't last."

Mohammed Ali's MOROCCO shirt blocked my view of the playing field.

"M'sieur you gonna play?"

"Uhh, no."

"How come, m'sieur?"

"I'd rather watch."

He went off to sit on the strip of grass bordering the turf. Ali turned the action back toward Sheik Omar, who was open on the left. He moved ahead to strike. The ball took off toward the top of an uncaring chestnut tree. The sixth graders gathered behind the goal went Oh. The ball dropped out of the tree in a rustle of leaves, then rolled toward the playing field as if by remote control.

With an unthinking kick, the adult goalie sent it toward a great friendly cloud, which refused to hold onto it, and the ball fell to his adolescent counterpart Jingbin, who with his hand sent it clumsily on to Baidi, who moved back toward the center circle and sent it to Ali, who passed it to Nassuif, who chipped it high over Mohammed the monitor and right at Sheik Omar, who head-butted the ball into the left top corner of the net above Serge, who, caught short without time to react, applauded and was imitated by Danièle.

"Even. Another one like that and we're finished."

A sixth-grader in a helmet hurled the ball to Luc, who, limping and holding his hip, brought it back to center field. Sheik Omar was already set to jump anyone who would take on the commitment. The task fell to Julien, who'd pulled back his hair with an elastic band and was catching his breath, his hands curled on his thighs. At the opposite goal, Jingbin held his hand flat above his eyes to shield them from the sun glittering in the enormous sky. Julien, doubled over, was delaying the outcome, while Baidi jumped around to let off steam.

END

ABOUT THE AUTHOR

FRANÇOIS BÉGAUDEAU is the author of two novels: *Jouer juste* (2003) and *Dans la diagonale* (2005). In 2005, he published a fictional biography of the Rolling Stones titled *Rolling Stones: Un démocrate Mick Jagger 1960–1969*. A film critic for the *Cahiers du cinema* and the French version of *Playboy*, he played in the punk band Zabriskie Point before becoming a teacher in France's public school system.

ABOUT THE TRANSLATOR

LINDA ASHER, a former fiction editor for the *New Yorker*, has translated into English Victor Hugo, Georges Simenon, and Milan Kundera. Her translations for Seven Stories Press include Martin Winckler's *The Case of Dr. Sachs* (*La maladie de Sachs*), which won the French-American Foundation Translation Prize in 2000; *Memoirs of a Breton Peasant*; and, most recently, *Evolution*.